A VIOLET WIND

KIT EARNSHAW

Edited by Madeline Concannon

Cover design by Roman Belopolsky

For Cricket

If you could read, I think you'd really like this story.

CHAPTER ONE

It was a Thursday night in the dead of winter, and we were having our weekly coven dinner. I was the host this week and had picked up some nice cheeses from the market to make a cheese board. I'd warned the girls it was going to be a lighter dinner. I didn't have it in me to cook that night. They understood and were more than happy to have a wine and cheese night. Coven dinner is really more about us spending time together and strengthening our bonds. The more emotionally and mentally connected a coven is, the stronger it is. One crack in the foundation, and your powers can begin to seep through and before you know it, you're empty.

The wine was free flowing as we tucked into the different cheeses— a creamy brie, a sharp and satisfying cheddar, a mild jarlsberg, and an earthy hard sheep's milk cheese. We were one-upping each other with our latest dating horror stories, when Hattie, with her eyes widened like a cartoon princess, asked us "Do you ever tell them you're a witch?" We burst out laughing. Hattie joined in. "I know, I know. . ."

Reina calmed her laughter and offered, "I did tell a guy once on a first date, just to see his reaction. Five minutes in and I knew it wasn't going anywhere so I thought what the hell, I'll fuck with this guy for a bit. Halfway through our drinks, I look him dead in the eyes and say, 'you should know something about me, I'm a witch.' He started laughing as if it was a joke— fair enough— so I double down and say 'No, seriously, I'm a practicing witch.' He looked so confused and then finally started asking the dumbest questions like 'Do I sacrifice goats? Can I predict the outcome of the superbowl? Is there a spell to make the Jets do better this season?'"

Bianca chimed in, "Let me guess, he lived in Murray Hill."

"Bingo." We all laughed until we groaned, because we had all been on dates with that type at some point. Former college athletes, finance bros, grown men still holding onto their fraternity days, they were all variations on the same theme. And a lot of them lived in Murray Hill. They never wanted to leave their glory days of college behind, so they continued them in the city, working the corporate grind until happy hour which inevitably led to lines of coke with their coworkers, and then more drinks, and if they were feeling fun, a karaoke room in K-town with more lines of coke and booze. Stumble home, pass out, wake up, rinse, repeat. I could usually spot these guys on the dating apps and would swipe left, but sometimes they were sneakier. It wasn't always obvious in their profile, but you'd make the discovery within the first fifteen minutes of your date.

"And this is why I date women," said Sage, her green eyes dancing in the candlelight as she smiled mischievously for effect.

"Ugh, I tried that already!" Hattie looked so defeated, it made us laugh even harder. "What?! I did!" But she started laughing too.

"Did you now, sweet thing?" Sage raised her eyebrows flirtily.

"Hattie, you have to tell her," I said.

"Violet," Hattie groaned, playfully rolling her eyes at me.

"Oh, so it's a whole story." Sage winked at me, and my stomach did a little flip.

"Story time!" Bianca cried out, raising her wine glass. We raised ours to meet hers and repeated, "Story time!" in a cheers.

"Fine," Hattie began. "I met this girl at a Yule party and thought she was so cute. I've never been with a woman before, though. After a few glasses of egg nog. . ."

"And a lot of dancing," added Bianca.

"Yes, a lot of dancing! We found ourselves making out on the couch in the corner, and I went home with her that night."

"Damn girl, zero to sixty!" Sage said.

"Yeah and we ended up dating for like a month."

"She was smitten, Hattie!" I said.

"So what happened, then?" asked Sage.

"She was telepathic and started to get intrusive. We'd be at a party or at a crowded bar, and she would just start chattering away in my brain or listening to my thoughts and would get jealous if my mind wandered to thoughts of someone else . . ." Hattie trailed off.

"And," Reina piped in, "you're leaving out the part that you were harboring a serious crush on our neighbor Nick that culminated in a one night stand."

"Okay, yeah, that was the bigger issue," Hattie said solemnly as she took a long sip of her wine, as the rest of us began to laugh. We were all giggly by that point from the heady amount of wine we'd consumed.

As I continued to stumble through my twenties, the coven was the one stabilizing force I clung to— my chosen sisters. I'd had Bianca by my side my whole life. Our mothers were in the same coven, so she'd always felt like family. Bianca was bright and bubbly and social, eager for adventure and new experiences. On our first big collegiate weekend at Greenwood Academy, she'd thrown a party in the basement of our dorm. That night we met Reina and Hattie, and our duo quickly became a quartet. We were inseparable for our four years at the academy, and after graduation, we moved to Brooklyn as a coven.

When I left the academy, I wasn't sure which path I wanted to take. . . my father wanted me to return to the normal world. The normal world being the world of the living, of the material, of the entirely human, flesh and blood. He wanted me to live a normal, conventional existence, like the one he had gone on to live when he and my mother split over a decade ago.

My mother, on the other hand, of course, was proud I graduated at the top of my class at the academy. I excelled at shadow work, clairsentience, tarot, exorcism, and magical anthropology. I'd even taken a semester to live with a commune of alchemists that eschewed technology in a secluded and snowy area of Canada and had my journals published in the underground press. I was making a name for myself in academia, and I wasn't even 21.

Without the structure of the academy though, I floundered. Now at 25, I was still learning to straddle these two worlds. I had space in myself to be both. I could hold a normal job, while still practicing magic. Sure, I didn't have a solid career path in mind yet, but at least I had my coven. To pay the bills, I worked at a bakery— not as a baker, that would be a lot cooler, but as a cashier. It was a good enough job I guess, but it wasn't like I was going to work there for the next thirty years. I wasn't really sure what I wanted to do with my life, other than spend it with my coven enjoying times like these.

Hattie was lounging on a worn magenta floor cushion and leaned back against Bianca, who was curled up in an old navy velvet armchair we'd found at a thrift store nearby. She began to play with Hattie's hair sweetly. Reina, Sage, and I were squeezed onto our faded pink couch. The candlelight cast the room in a golden glow, and I could feel myself smiling moonily.

Next to me, Sage leaned forward to grab a cracker and smeared some brie on it. She leaned back as she munched contentedly, resting a hand on my leg. I felt a tingle run through my body. I glanced around making sure nobody noticed. They didn't. It wasn't out of the ordinary. As a coven, we were affectionate with each other, but I usually didn't feel this kind of energy flowing through my body when Bianca or Reina or Hattie touched me. I took a quick gulp of wine, determined to let it go and stay in the moment. If that meant I needed a stronger buzz, so be it. We still had a whole bottle of wine left.

SAGE LARSEN WAS the newest member of our coven. Bianca had met her one autumn evening at an underground lounge in the West Village. They ended up talking for three hours over dirty martinis and became fast friends. I began to hear Sage's name thrown around the apartment more and more; she was enamored.

At 28, Sage was a couple years older than us and had been entrenched in the city's magical community for a decade. She had opened her own metaphysical shop a few years ago, and Bianca would spend her free time on the weekends perusing the store for hours. She'd return laden with new crystals, books, and herbs for us to use. Finally, Bianca introduced her to us. She'd asked if Sage could join us for a Full Moon ritual, and we cautiously agreed. The four of us had been together since our first year at the academy. How would a fifth person affect our dynamic?

When Sage showed up to our apartment that Full Moon, I instantly understood Bianca's infatuation. Sage was magnetic. She was physically striking, with close cropped hair dyed a pastel turquoise, big round eyes the color of moss, and a heart shaped mouth that rested in a perpetual devilish smirk. She looked like she was always on the verge of laughter, as if there was some inside joke to which we weren't privy.

"Hi, I'm Sage. Thank you so much for having me," she said, her voice crystalline and soothing like the steady fall of rain in summer. She hugged each of us, and as we embraced, I felt a warm tingle on the back of my neck. A faint smell of vetiver and lavender emanated from her parchment-colored skin.

"I brought you all something," she said, as she reached into her canvas tote bag. One by one, she pulled out a shimmering royal blue obelisk for each of us. "Lapis lazuli is one of my favorite stones," she commented, as she handed over the palm-sized crystals. She gingerly placed it in my open hand, her green eyes sparkling as she met my gaze.

"Thank you, this is so thoughtful," I said as I curled my fingers around the obelisk. A faint pulse began to beat behind my third eye point as I held it.

That night lives like a joyful blur in my memory now. We danced on the rooftop under mother moon's light until we entered a trance, the corporeal world melting away as we reached a higher plane. Spirits spoke to us and visions played before our eyes. We chanted an incantation to light a fire only we could see and feel, its embers sparkling in the night.

As time crept on, we howled at the moon and heard a distant reply of wolves. Our eyes grew wide as we listened to their call, likely being sounded by a pack of lycanthropes enjoying their monthly respite from humanity. We began to laugh, throwing our heads back, cheeks kissed rosy by the chill in the air. In the wee hours of the morning, I crawled into my bed and fell into a deep slumber for thirteen hours. I awoke the next morning with my hand tightly clasping the lapis lazuli obelisk Sage had given me. She was now one of us, a sister and a friend.

THE MORNING AFTER COVEN DINNER, I bundled up in my long black puffy coat with a big faux fur hood that made me feel like I was a tundra princess. I trekked into Williamsburg to grab a coffee before work at Three of Cups. It was a popular underground haunt that served up coffee during daylight and booze after dark. Not everyone who frequented Three of Cups was part of the underground scene. Normal humans would pop in for coffee or a beer, but the majority of the clientele had a special bend to them.

The door swung open wildly as I entered the cafe, and I wasn't sure if it was from the gust of wind or my own power. I'd chalk it up to the wind, but sometimes things like doors swinging open or windows shutting on their own happens around me. I'd suddenly realize I was getting too cold from the draft coming in from the window, and it would quickly shut, or I'd be excited to walk into a bar that my friends were waiting in, and the door would swing open on its own without me having to push. Nothing crazy, just a little spooky maybe.

I noticed the music was immediately different from the usual low fi indie pop or '70s folk songs they'd often play depending on who was behind the counter. "Paradise City" by Guns N' Roses was playing loudly, and I started to laugh. The barista turned around to face me and said "What? It's a jam. And maybe I'm playing it ironically." My heart stopped, and I felt like I'd had the wind knocked out of me. I had never seen this man before but he was gorgeous. He was probably 6 feet tall with long muscular arms bulging out from under his ratty olive green t-shirt. His light brown hair was peeking out from underneath a heathered grey beanie. He had bright grey eyes and a playful smile. Our eyes locked, and his cheeks began to flush. "Sorry, do I know you?" he asked.

"No? I don't think so. . . are you new?"

"Yeah, this is my first week. I'm Jackson."

"Violet."

"Nice to meet you, Violet. What can I get you?" He smiled as he cocked his head to the side, surveying me. I couldn't look away from him.

"Um," I stammered. "Sorry, my mind has gone totally blank."

His smile widened, and he let out a soft laugh. "No rush, I get it." He paused before adding, "I like your coat."

"Thanks. . . um, I'll just have coffee with cream, please." I reached into my bag and then handed him my reusable thermos to fill. It was one of my tiny efforts to fight climate change. Maybe all the paper coffee cups and plastic lids I was saving didn't have a huge impact, but hey, it helped my conscience feel a little better.

"Coming right up." He winked at me before turning around to pour my coffee. I inhaled slowly, trying to collect myself. Was he a witch? Or a clairvoyant? He could be any number of things; he could be human for all I knew. I don't know why I was having such a strong reaction to him. . . and could he tell? Was he feeling it too?

Jackson cleared his throat, pulling me out of my head and back into the cafe. "One coffee with cream." He handed me my thermos back, and my fingertips grazed his as I took the cup. My hand felt like it was just shocked, and I could swear he felt it too. He looked at me with eyes wide, his mouth half open as if to say something.

"Thanks," I said, continuing to stand there with

my thermos. My brain felt foggy, and my body felt like it was moving through molasses.

"Uh, yeah, can I order please?" said a voice from behind me.

Jackson and I both burst out laughing, and I stepped aside and apologized to a mohawked woman in combat boots that was glaring at me. "Sorry," I said through my laughter. She rolled her eyes.

"Oh! I forgot to pay!"

"Seriously?" Mohawk said, dripping with annoyance.

"It's on the house." Jackson said before helping Mohawk.

I grabbed my wallet and found two dollar bills that I stuffed into the tip jar before heading back into the cold. I didn't let myself catch Jackson's eye. I needed a moment to recenter myself before heading to the bakery.

IT WAS a quiet afternoon at the bakery. Snow had begun to fall, coating the sidewalks in an icy frosting, deterring most people from venturing outside. I sat behind the counter on a wooden stool reading a tattered copy of Agatha Christie's *The Murder at the Vicarage*. I'd found a big box of her books outside a stoop on Guernsey Street marked free and lugged them all home. One of my favorite things about Greenpoint was how often I stumbled across piles of free books. It was like happening upon a surprise library.

The bell on the door rang out loudly announcing a customer. "Hey," said a familiar voice. I looked up from my book to see Sage.

"Hey!" I stood up and walked out from behind the counter to give her a hug. Immediately, I was struck by that heady mix of vetiver and lavender. "Can I get you anything? What are you up to?"

She ignored both of my questions and eyed the novel atop the counter where I'd left it. "I love Miss Marple," she commented.

"Me too," I agreed. "What are you doing in the neighborhood?"

"I just really wanted to see where you worked. You're so coy about it," Sage said, her mossy eyes glinting mischievously.

"I don't mean to be . . . I guess I just feel like I should be doing something more than manning the counter at a bakery." Sage studied my face pensively. "Do you want a cinnamon roll? They're kind of what we're known for here," I added.

"Sure," she said. I gingerly grabbed a bulbous cinnamon roll from the case and plated it. I handed her the plate, and she took a big bite of the cinnamon roll. Her already big round eyes grew twice their size as she chewed smiling.

"Oh my god, this is incredible. I think my mouth just had an orgasm." We both laughed as she took another bite.

"I told you," I said. "Best cinnamon rolls in all of Brooklyn."

"My regards to the baker . . . is she one of us?"

"Nope, there's not an ounce of magic in that baby," I said, gesturing to the roll as Sage took another hungry bite.

"Wow," she mused as she chewed blissfully. Her whole face was glowing happily. Sage radiated joy. I had yet to see her sad or angry. When she entered a room, she bathed everything and everyone in her light. She was powerful, I could tell. "You know, you shouldn't be ashamed or embarrassed or whatever about working here," she said as she set down the plate with one big bite left. "And don't take that away, I'm saving that bite."

"I don't know . . ." I trailed off, unsure of what to say.

"What would you rather be doing?" Sage asked.

"I don't know! That's the thing. At the academy, it was so easy. I had all these options, and I could excel and be acknowledged for my talents and my hard work. Every course was laid out for me. I knew how to be successful. If I followed the syllabus, listened to the professor, and did what was expected of me, I was praised."

"So you were a real color-in-the-lines kind of kid," Sage interjected with a joking smile.

I laughed. "Maybe, but I think it was more that I felt like that praise validated my existence. I belonged. I was a part of something bigger at the academy."

Sage paused thoughtfully as she took me in, surveying me with those shining green eyes. I let her. She wasn't scrutinizing me, she was reading me in a way that felt like she was caring for me. I wanted to be seen by her. I felt safe. "That makes sense . . . but you have the coven now."

I nodded, "That's true. I'm definitely happiest when we are all together, even if we're not doing magic."

"You know, I didn't go to Greenwood Academy or any of the underground colleges like it," Sage said.

"You didn't?" I was surprised. Maybe I shouldn't have assumed she'd attended university like the rest of us, but it hadn't occurred to me you could be such an actualized witch without proper training and study.

"No, everything I learned I did on my own. I was a hedge witch having to teach myself magic. I devoured any book I could find and would practice late at night in my bedroom with the door closed."

"I'm sorry," I said.

Sage smiled. "Why are you sorry?"

"I don't know, I guess that just sounds lonely."

"It really wasn't. I had my friends at school, and I skipped out on regular college and moved to Brooklyn after high school and found other witches and the underground scene."

"What about your family?" I asked. I was realizing I didn't know anything about Sage's life.

"Well, my dad was really supportive. He's not a witch, but my mother was. She died when I was five."

"I'm so sorry. That must have been really hard," I

wanted to reach out and hold Sage and stroke her turquoise head like a mother would.

She just shrugged and said matter-of-factly, "Thanks, but I was so young. And my dad and I are really close." I nodded as she popped the last bite of cinnamon roll into her heart-shaped mouth to savor.

CHAPTER TWO

"You really should get the White Negroni," said Dave emphatically, as he eyed me from across the table.

"No thanks, I really want the Frozen Painkiller," I said, fighting the urge to roll my eyes.

"But isn't it a little cold for frozen drinks?" This guy wasn't going to let up.

"Well, we're inside and the heat is on. I think I'll be fine. Thank you for your concern though," I said, somehow keeping my expression completely serene. He got the hint, though, and nodded curtly before walking to the bar.

It was my second date with Dave. He was tall and good-looking, if a little generic. His dark brown hair was carefully coiffed, and his olive skin was perfectly bronzed from a vacation to Turks and Caicos. He'd just returned and couldn't stop talking about how fantastic it had been to be able to get away and just relax on the beach, soaking up the sun's rays. "You know how it is, gotta get out when New York gets dismal like this. Maybe I have seasonal depression," he joked. I didn't laugh. He didn't need to be fooled into thinking I found him funny or charming. Dave had plenty of women indulging him already, I was sure of it.

On our first date, he'd prefaced the evening with "Just so you know, I am seeing other women and looking to just have fun in Q1." Yes, he spoke finance to me. I wasn't looking for love or anything serious either, so that suited me fine. He'd managed to get a table last minute at a hot new tapas restaurant in the West Village and had no problem dropping his black credit card with a heavy thud on the bill.

Hattie didn't understand why I was wasting my time going on dates with Dave, but we were polar opposites when it came to matters of the heart. She wanted to find her soulmate, someone that completed her body, mind, and spirit. That sounded great but unrealistic to me. I'd seen how love could fade and relationships could destroy a person, leaving them swimming in the wake of emotional wreckage. I didn't need that pain. But I did need sex. And Dave was gorgeous, like objectively good looking in that tall, dark, and handsome way. He was proud of his body and showed it off confidently in the bedroom. I slept with him that first date, and when he undressed, he stood before me, as if inviting me to admire his carefully chiseled physique.

The sex was mediocre, though. There had been some light kissing and awkward foreplay. He couldn't seem to find my clit. Even if I'd handed him a map and flashlight, he'd still be a millimeter off. I had been too tipsy on Dom Perignon to correct him. After some perfunctory thrusting, he came in his condom and apologized for being unable to bring me to climax and promised me he'd make it up to me. So here I was, letting him make it up to me.

Dave set down the drinks and shook his head disapprovingly as he handed me the Frozen Painkiller. I took a sip and let its icy sweetness trickle down my throat like nectar. "It's delicious," I said, blissfully happy with my choice. Dave looked mildly miffed.

"I can't imagine drinking anything frozen right now. Might as well drink snow," he remarked. "Plus, I got my fill of frozen bevies in Turks." He let out a deep self-satisfied chuckle. Oh, life was so easy for Dave. "Do you have a favorite island in the Caribbean?" Was he really asking me this question? I resisted the urge to laugh at his ridiculousness and just shook my head instead.

"No, I can't say that I do," I said.

"Too many to choose from, I know. And each just has that little special thing that just makes them so unique, you know?" For Dave, he was waxing poetic, and I couldn't fight my annoyance any longer.

"No, actually, I don't know. I can't really afford those kinds of trips. I went to Puerto Rico once with my family and the Bahamas with a few girlfriends once, and they were both lovely trips, but I get the feeling your Caribbean experiences are very different," I said.

"Ah, don't be a sourpuss now," he said with a cocky smile. "Maybe if you're a good girl, I'll take you one day." Gross. Instead of sassing him back, I just began to suck down my Painkiller in a steady rhythm. He continued to talk about his trip as my attention faded. I kept my eyes trained on the dwindling pale yellow slush until it disappeared completely.

AFTER MY SECOND PAINKILLER, I was feeling considerably more flirty. Maybe horny was the more appropriate word. As Dave talked about work and the gym, I admired his full, tan lips, the sexy chocolate scruff on his square jaw, his thick black lashes that lined his deep mahogany eyes. He could be so dreamy, if only he didn't talk. But guys like Dave were a dime a dozen in New York City. They weren't always tall or muscular or rich, but they were always extraordinarily confident and self-centered.

I extended my hand across the table and began to trace my finger along his open palm, nodding along to whatever he was saying. His hands were big and smooth, the hands of someone who had never done an ounce of manual labor. "Your hands are so soft," I murmured coyly as I flashed him a small smile.

"Oh yeah?" he asked with a devilish grin. I nodded as I pouted my red lacquered lips. "Should we see what I can do with these hands? Maybe go somewhere a little more private?" I nodded again.

"I'd love that," I said, pushing my chest slightly forward. My low-cut sheer sweater clung to my bra, as Dave's eyes trailed to my cleavage. He licked his lips absentmindedly, before announcing he would close out the tab.

I pulled my phone out while he was paying our bill at the bar. There was a text from Bianca: *Hey, how's the date? Hope the sex is better this time LOL.* I smiled and quickly typed out my response. *He's so boring but the drinks are good haha. Heading to his place now.* I slipped my phone back into my black leather tote as Dave approached the table.

"Shall we?" he asked, standing over me.

"We shall," I said as I put on my coat and wrapped my neck in the plum-colored woolen scarf Hattie had knitted me for Yule.

As we began to walk down the block, heading towards Dave's place, my name suddenly pierced the air. "Violet?" I turned to see who had called out to me.

The barista from Three of Cups was standing bundled in a thick, puffy jacket and snug black beanie under the awning of a sushi restaurant. "Jackson?" I asked, as if I wasn't sure of his name even though it was seared into my memory. He flashed a wide smile and nodded, his bright grey eyes shining like silver in the neon glow from the restaurant's Sapporo sign. His cheeks were rosy from the cold air, and I imagined cupping his face in my hands to warm them.

"I'm just waiting for a friend," he offered. We continued to smile at each other until Dave cleared his throat loudly.

"We should really get going," Dave said.

"Oh, right, well have a good night, Jackson," I said.

"You too, Violet," he said. I looked into his silvery eyes one last time before walking away with Dave. I wondered who he was meeting for dinner. Was he on a date? Did he think Dave was my boyfriend? God, I hoped not.

We walked the three blocks to Dave's place and headed up to his apartment. He lived in a newer building, with a doorman and elevators and rooftop deck with lounge chairs and a grill. It must have cost double my apartment, which was a third floor walkup in a pre-war building. No doorman, no air-conditioning, no amenities.

The minute we opened the door to his unit, he peeled off his coat. I followed suit, and he began kissing me fervently. We were off to the races. As we kissed, he grabbed my ass hard, pulling me into him. I felt an anticipatory thrill run down my spine as I began to fumble with his shirt's buttons. He lifted my thin sweater up over my head, his eyes feasting on my light pink nipples as they peeked through the lace of my bra. Dave licked his lips then kissed me hungrily. I ran my hand down his taut bare chest, feeling every ripple of hard-earned muscle until I reached his pants. Underneath, he was stiff and ready. I lightly teased the fabric as he grunted.

He undid his belt and dropped his pants before tugging on my black mini skirt and tights, pulling them to the floor. With only our underwear left, we began to furiously make out as he led me to his bedroom and onto his bed. He clumsily unhooked my bra and tossed it aside as he grabbed greedily at each plump breast. I slid his soft cotton boxer briefs off, and his erection sprung free, poking me in the abdomen. He quickly yanked off my lace thong and began to touch me. I waited as he felt around, stroking here and there but never landing on the right spot. I shifted my hips, trying to guide him. I began to get frustrated. "It's right here," I said finally, grabbing his hand and placing it on my clit.

"Yeah, I know," he said. I rolled my eyes before leaning back so I could try and enjoy his fingering. Jackson's grey eyes suddenly came into focus, and I began to imagine his lips on mine, his fingers inside me instead of Dave's. I sighed, which Dave mistook as encouraging.

"Don't drift," I remarked, looking down. He'd already lost my clit again. He grunted and found it as he began to stroke it faster, kissing my inner thigh before placing his lips at the crest of my opening. He licked without skill or finesse. I looked up at the ceiling. I just wanted to cum, but Dave was making it hard, no pun intended.

"This isn't working," I announced. He stopped and looked up at me.

"What?" he asked confusedly. "We can switch it up then. Let me get a condom." He stood up and went to his dresser.

I got off the bed and began to collect my clothing, putting it back on. "No," I said. "I'm just not into this, Dave. I've gotta go."

He looked shell shocked, as if someone had died. Had he really never been turned down before?

"You're serious? You're really leaving?" he asked incredulously.

"Yeah . . . thanks for the drinks." I said, quickly kissing his cheek and grabbing my coat, scarf, and bag on the way out. He was so stunned he didn't move from that spot. In the elevator, I began to bundle up for the cold trip back to Brooklyn. I was glad to be free of Dave but still incredibly sexually frustrated. Bianca was going to think this was hilarious when I told her later.

———

SAGE TEXTED me on my day off and asked if I wanted to grab a coffee at Three of Cups. I was buzzing with excitement so I wasn't surprised when the door blew open forcefully as I approached, even though the air was still. I stuck out my arm to make it look like I'd pushed it open purposefully in case anyone was watching. It was bustling for a weekday afternoon. Every seat at the long wooden communal table was occupied by people typing away on their laptops. I looked towards the back of the shop and saw Sage had snagged a spot on one of the caramel colored leather couches. She waved at me and smiled.

"Violet!" I turned to see who had called my name. It was Jackson. My stomach did a little flip. He was smiling at me warmly. His plaid flannel shirt was bunched up around the elbows, punctuating the bulge of his strong forearms. His long slender fingers were pulling an espresso shot for the customer waiting at the counter.

"Hey, Jackson," I said.

"What are you up to today?" he asked as he handed the man his shot of espresso. The guy gave him a few dollars and walked back to his armchair by the window.

"I'm just meeting my friend Sage for coffee," I said, gesturing towards the leather couch.

"Cool, I like her hair."

"Yeah, me too." I couldn't seem to break eye contact with him, but I also couldn't think of anything to say.

"So what can I get you? Coffee with cream again?" I nodded.

"Do you live in the neighborhood?" I asked, thankful a question had popped into my head.

"Nope, I'm in Bushwick. What about you?"

"Greenpoint, so not far."

"I love Greenpoint. Do you ever eat at that Polish place with the mannequins out front?"

"Sometimes, but I usually order Polish food in.

And I cannot for the life of me pronounce any of the restaurant names."

"It's a lot of consonants, isn't it?" He laughed, and I nodded, smiling.

He handed me a big china mug of creamy coffee. Our fingers touched, deliberately this time. He let his hand rest next to mine for longer than necessary as my fingers curled around the cup. We looked at each other intently. I swear I could feel his pulse quicken in his fingertips, and my own hand tingled with an electricity that began to travel up my arm. I pulled back, unsure of what was happening. I looked around to see if anyone had noticed. Nobody had. I glanced at Sage, who was engrossed in one of the old astrology books they kept on the coffee table by the couch.

Jackson kept his silvery eyes on me and inhaled slowly. "Could I have your number?" he asked.

"What?" I hadn't expected that.

"Your number? For a date?"

"Oh, of course." I let out a little giggle, but inside I was dancing. A parade of butterflies was marching from my stomach to my heart as I dug through my black leather tote to find my notepad and pen. I quickly scribbled down my name and number before tearing it out and handing it over.

"Thanks," he said, looking down at the scrap of paper with a small smile.

I nodded and made my way towards Sage. I nestled in next to her on the couch as she set down the thick astrology book she had been reading. "I love that one," she remarked, running her nimble fingers over the faded cover. "What did you get?"

"Just a coffee with cream, you?"

"Green tea." She picked up her mug and took a long sip. I watched the steam unfurl in front of her nose. She had a smattering of pale freckles across the bridge of her nose. I hadn't noticed them before now. She looked up at me as she set her cup back down. "What?" she asked.

"Sorry, I just was noticing your freckles. They're really sweet."

"No need to apologize. Thanks. I hated them as a kid. They'd get so dark in the summer, I thought my face looked like a speckled egg. I love them now though." She took another contented sip of her tea, as I continued to visually map her freckles like a facial cartographer.

"You know, our names are both colors," Sage mused as she folded her legs underneath her on the couch. "Violet and Sage."

"They're also both plants," I said.

"Oh, you're right," Sage smiled absentmindedly as her eyes wandered around the coffee shop.

CHAPTER THREE

I was getting ready to meet Jackson for our first date. He'd called like he said he would and immediately asked me to brunch on Saturday. I hadn't ever been on a date during the day. My standard first date was a couple drinks at a bar where I could use alcohol to either make myself less anxious and more interesting, or more often, my date more interesting. It might not be the healthiest approach to dating, but it was the best way I'd found to handle the frustrations and disappointments of the New York City dating scene.

Bianca sat on my bed watching me put my makeup on as she talked about a guy she met the other night at our favorite underground bar, The Tilted Hollow. "Okay, so he's a super hot demonologist— bald with a ginger beard, so sexy. God, I love the confidence of a bald man."

"Did you get his number?" I asked as I carefully ran the mascara wand through my curled lashes.

"No," Bianca said with a frustrated exhale.

"We'll have to go back then. I can wingwoman you."

"Yes! Please! I feel like he goes there a lot," she said with a smirk.

I finished my makeup with one last swipe of coral blush on each cheek bone. I turned around to face Bianca. "How do I look?"

"Gorgeous. He's gonna die when he sees you." I was so nervous, it felt like there was a thunderstorm in my stomach. I'd never been this worked up over a first date, and Bianca could tell. "Vi, it's gonna be fine. Just be yourself and have fun." I nodded as I began to put on my favorite grey suede ankle booties with the three-inch heel that gave me an extra boost of confidence.

"Here, wear this for good luck." Bianca slid her dainty rose quartz bracelet off of her wrist. She held out her hand, asking for mine. I reached my left arm out and she took my hand gently in hers and glided the sweet pink bracelet onto my wrist. I felt the tightness in my chest immediately relax and the thunder in my belly calm. I took a deep breath as I let Bianca's charm take effect on me. It was immediately evident that she'd programmed the crystals with some kind of anti-anxiety magic. I wonder if she had planned for this.

"Better?" she asked.

"Much, thanks." I hugged her tightly.

"I have a good feeling about this," she whispered

into my ear before letting go. I smiled and nodded as I put on my coat.

THE DOOR BLEW open just as my fingertips were about to touch it and immediately my nostrils were filled with the scent of freshly brewed coffee and bacon grease. Jackson had picked a cozy spot off the beaten path in South Williamsburg. I was glad we wouldn't have to wait for a table, as I spotted him already seated at a small table for two next to a flickering fire. He stood up when he spotted me and smiled, his grey eyes crinkling warmly. We hugged, and he kissed me on the cheek. He smelled faintly of cedar and amber. It was intoxicating and I had to stop myself from huffing him like a drug. I could still feel the heat of his lips on my cold windswept cheek as I sat down across from him.

"I can't believe this place has an actual fireplace," I said.

"I know, I'm trying to keep it a secret. I don't ever want to have to battle a crowd to come here."

"It's so nice," I remarked as I watched the flames dance.

"You look beautiful." His eyes were fixed on me intently. He raised his brows slightly, as if to make sure it was okay he had complimented me.

"Thank you, that's sweet. You're not so bad yourself." I laughed awkwardly and he smiled.

Jackson told me they were known for their Eggs Benedict and homemade pastries. The waiter brought us a blueberry muffin and an almond croissant to share while we sipped our coffee. I tore off a bite of almond croissant and let it melt in my mouth. My eyes closed in bliss.

"It's good, right?" asked Jackson as he chewed a bite of muffin before continuing to tell me about his apartment in Bushwick.

"It's just this massive loft, but we've made it cozy. And I feel lucky that I get to live with so many of my friends," he said.

"There's 6 of you total, and you all manage to get along?" I asked in disbelief.

He let out a low chuckle. "Yeah, I mean, we have our moments, but for the most part, everything is copacetic."

The waiter dropped our entrees, warning us of their hot plates. I had ordered the Eggs Norwegian, the Benedict made with smoked salmon, while Jackson had ordered their classic Benedict. We immediately dug in. I munched contentedly as I listened to Jackson passionately talk about playing the guitar. I couldn't stop staring at his hands. I could tell they were strong from years of playing, with long, agile fingers.

"So, you want to be a musician, then, I take it? I mean, you are a musician, clearly, but you want it to be your career?" I asked.

"Yeah, definitely. I've booked little gigs here and there with my band, but picked up those shifts at Three of Cups to make some extra cash," he said as he pierced a bit of ham with his fork.

"What about your family, though? Where are you from?" He changed the subject, and I wasn't sure I liked the new topic.

"I'm from a small town upstate. My parents are divorced," I said plainly.

"What about siblings? Do you get along with your parents?" Jackson's bright grey eyes searched my face for answers, and I wasn't great at giving them. Shit.

"I'm an only child. I love my parents. The divorce happened when I was a teenager. It was sad, but ultimately for the best. I have good relationships with both of them, so it all worked out in the end." I rattled it off mechanically. It was my usual response to this question. I didn't get into the nitty gritty of how my father resented my mother because she wouldn't eschew her powers or talents for him after her strength began to wear on him after so many years. Or that when I hit adolescence, my own unpredictable power and teenage hormones only amplified the tension in our house.

I was so protective of my parents, even though my relationships with each of them had been strained at times. My father wasn't a bad man for resenting my mother, and my mother wasn't selfish for choosing her magic over him and our little family of three. When I was a teenager, I'd go through phases where I thought those things, sometimes siding with my father and other times staunchly standing by my mother's side. As I'd grown into adulthood, I'd begun to understand more clearly just how complicated relationships and people were, regardless of magic getting in the way.

"What about your family? Your parents still together?" I asked him before taking a bite of lox.

"Yep, they're still going strong. I actually grew up on a farm in Pennsylvania. They still live there with my youngest sister. I'm the oldest of four." He paused briefly for a sip of coffee before continuing, "I'm the only boy, but we're all really close. The oldest of the girls, Fiona, is actually one of my roommates."

"Oh wow, you *are* close," I remarked. It sounded nice and warm, a farm full of love, happy parents, happy children.

"Yeah," he said, smiling sheepishly. "Is that not sexy?" he asked jokingly.

I began to laugh and shook my head. "No, I think it sounds really nice. Idyllic, really. It was kind of lonely sometimes growing up without siblings." The bonds of siblinghood were utterly foreign to me. I didn't have anyone to share the unique experience of growing up in my family. Nobody but me knew what it was like to be raised by my mother and father.

"Ah well, it wasn't *that* idyllic. I mean, I love my family and I had a great childhood, but we had our problems just like any other family." He paused and looked me in the eye. I couldn't break away from his gaze. It was like looking into two swirling silver pools of light, like how the moon reflects off of the ripples in the East River just after the sun has set on a cloudy day. We sat like that in silence for a few minutes, just looking at each other thoughtfully. It was vulnerable, but I wasn't uncomfortable. I was surprised by how safe I felt around him, actually. I wasn't searching for questions to ask to make the date go by more quickly or throwing back drinks to make it more interesting.

The waiter came by and dropped the check, pulling our awareness back into the restaurant. It was starting to fill up, and I could tell they needed to turn the table. Jackson quickly scooped up the bill and gave the waiter his card. I thanked him, but he brushed it off before asking if I wanted to grab a coffee.

"You need more caffeine?" I asked, and he laughed and rolled his eyes.

"No, I just want to spend more time with you. I'm really enjoying this." He smiled sincerely. He was oddly earnest. Maybe it wasn't odd, maybe I was just jaded by being single and in the city dating scene for too long.

"I am too," I agreed.

"Great, let's grab another coffee and take a walk around the neighborhood."

WE STROLLED TO DOMINO PARK, a strip of urban oasis that hugged the East River, as we sipped our coffee. I curled my fingers tightly around the cup, willing it to keep my hand warm. The air was crisp and cold, but the sun was bright and illuminated the dirty snow banks that were left from last week's snowfall. Despite the temperature, it was a gorgeous, cloudless winter day. We talked about music and our favorite bands. Jackson's tastes were eclectic. He loved everything from vaporwave to indie pop to jazz. There wasn't a single kind of music that he didn't seem to appreciate. I listened as he waxed poetically about the chord progression of a song he'd been working on. "So what about you, though?" he asked.

"What about me?"

"Well I've been talking your ear off about music... what makes you excited?"

I took a moment to think about my answer. A lot of things make me excited. And I certainly couldn't go into detail about witchcraft and my coven. "You know, I really love to dance." It sounded lame the minute I said it. I liked to dance? That's what excited me? It wasn't like I was a trained ballerina.

But Jackson was all in. "Really? What kind of dance?"

"Any kind I guess. I just love to dance. I love the way music feels in my body and how a song can dictate how I move without me thinking about it. It gets me out of head. And it just feels so damn good."

He laughed and agreed. "I love to dance too. I know exactly what you mean. We should go dancing sometime."

"Yeah?" I looked up at him hopefully.

"Definitely," he said with a smile.

We stopped to look out at the skyline jutting out majestically over the East River. The sunlight danced across the tops of skyscrapers, reflecting off the glass windows like a series of disco balls.

"I feel like I'm looking at a city for ants. Everything looks small and crowded from here. There are so many people packed onto that narrow little island." He turned to face me, angling his chin down to see me better. "What?" I asked.

"I just like listening to you talk." He paused for a moment. "And also, I'd really like to kiss you." I could feel my cheeks getting hot and the butterflies began to thunder in my stomach. I looked at his lips. They were pale pink and looked soft. He was smiling slightly.

"I think you should kiss me then," I said.

Without a beat, he leaned in and pressed his lips into mine. I felt like I was going to explode as he placed one hand on my waist and cupped my face in the other. It was like electricity shot through me, surging from his mouth and his hands into my body. He gave my waist a little squeeze and kissed me harder, slightly parting his lips so our tongues could meet. I began to tingle as I wrapped my arms around him, kissing him deeply. Every inch of me wanted more, but I didn't want to get carried away for all of Domino Park to see. We pulled apart slowly, but held hands as we smiled moonily at each other. I felt like a teenager again, adrenaline and lust coursing through my veins.

Suddenly we were interrupted as a voice from behind me shouted, "Jackson!" I saw a flash of recognition cross Jackson as he broke his gaze away from mine. I turned around to see who had called his name. A tall woman with thick long auburn hair was striding towards us confidently. She wore tight black jeans that were artfully distressed and an oversized leather biker jacket over a cream chunky knit sweater.

"Athena, hey," said Jackson.

"Hey," she said, looking me up and down.

"Athena, this is Violet." Jackson said as he put his hand on the small of my back. I thought I could feel his pulse for a second. It felt like it was reverberating through my body. "Athena is one of my roommates," he explained.

"Oh, hi. Nice to meet you," I said.

Her eyes narrowed as she cocked her head to the side, surveying me. What was her issue? Was this chick always this rude?

"What are you doing here?" Jackson asked. "I thought you were working today."

"I'm working tonight. I swapped shifts with someone. And it was such a gorgeous day I thought I'd come down and sit by the water." She didn't break eye contact with Jackson. I realized there was something between them. It may have been one sided, but there was definitely more to their relationship than just being roommates.

"Well, it's a gorgeous day for that," Jackson said.

"Isn't it just?" She smirked as Jackson took my hand in his and gave it a little tug.

"We should get going. I'll see you at home, Athena."

"See you tonight," she said as she watched us walk away from her.

When we were out of earshot, Jackson apologized. I told him he didn't need to and that he had nothing to be sorry about. "Well, she was being rude," he said.

"I think it has something to do with you," I said.

"She's just protective. We've known each other a long time; she's practically family."

"Okay," I said, shrugging it off. He squeezed my hand as if to reassure me, and we kept walking.

CHAPTER FOUR

We ended up at a nondescript dive bar on the border of Williamsburg and Greenpoint. It had a retro feel to it— wood panelled walls adorned with vintage beer ads and old Tiffany-style lamps hung above the bar. Their stained glass shades cast a romantic glow across the room. Jackson and I sat side by side at the end of the bar, our legs touching. He had one hand on his pint glass and the other rested on my knee. All I wanted to do was kiss him. The feeling of his leg against mine, his hand on my knee, made my whole body feel like it was humming. We had been talking at the bar for over an hour. And I couldn't stop staring at his lips as he talked, his perfectly soft lips. I was trying not to get distracted by my overwhelming lust, but I couldn't shake the electric current that would flow into me every time he touched me.

"Can you feel that?" I asked, looking down at his hand on my knee. "Am I crazy? Do you feel that?"

He tilted his head to the side and gave my knee a little squeeze before trailing his fingertips further up my thigh. The electricity intensified and my eyes bulged at him. He bit his lip, that pouty lip, and then gave me a sly smile.

"I feel everything you're feeling," he said before leaning in and kissing me deeply. My stomach flipped with excitement. "I haven't been able to stop thinking about you since I first saw you that morning in Three of Cups."

"Really?" I asked. So it hadn't been in my head, he had felt that energy between us.

"You came into the cafe that morning like a force of nature. I felt like I'd been stunned. I had never seen someone so beautiful," he said earnestly, looking me square in the eyes. Normally, a line like that would leave me rolling my eyes, but I could tell it wasn't a line Jackson was throwing around in hopes of getting laid. He was so sincere.

I leaned into him and pressed my lips lightly against his, kissing him softly. "I've never felt so connected to a stranger before, Jackson. I think I knew you in a past life."

He brushed my loose hair behind my ear with his long slender fingers. "I would believe it."

We finished our beers, but neither of us wanted to say goodbye. Jackson suggested we grab dinner at a taco place nearby. We ate ravenously as we told stories from our childhood.

"Well this," Jackson said, pointing to his adorably crooked nose, "happened in middle school. My sister

Fiona, the one that lives with me now, was bullied incessantly by this group of boys. I mean, they were relentless. And one day, I just snapped. I began walloping them— all three of them. I got my nose broken, and they ended up covered in bruises. But they never bothered Fi again. They realized if I could take them on like that, one versus three, the tormenting wasn't worth the risk." He smiled proudly.

"Little did they know, your nose would become part of your charm," I said with a flirtatious smirk.

"Oh yeah? It's charming now, is it?" he asked in a faux-coy voice.

"Very…" I said as he grinned.

"What about you? Ever break any bones?"

"Yes, my arm in the second grade," I began. "The Olympics had been on that summer and I became obsessed with gymnastics. I was a fearless and reckless child, so naturally I began to attempt the gymnastics I'd seen on the TV in my backyard." Jackson's eyes widened in anticipation. It was easy to see where this was going. I started to laugh. "I jumped off my wooden playset and somersaulted through the air, only to land on my arm."

"Damn, that's hardcore," he said with a laugh.

"Oh yeah, and I got a kickass cast that everyone signed."

"I was always jealous of those kids. It looked so cool."

"Very cool, but very itchy," I said with a solemn shake of the head. His laughter filled the air and warmed me like a hug. Jackson had one of those special laughs that was so genuine and reassuring, it felt like wearing my favorite sweater.

WHEN WE FINISHED EATING, I asked Jackson if he wanted to come back to my place for a nightcap. He smiled and said he'd love to, so we held hands as I walked us back to my apartment. I knew Bianca was out for drinks with Reina at The Tilted Hollow, hoping to run into that ginger-bearded demonologist again, so we would have the place to ourselves.

"I'm excited to see your place," he said as I unlocked the apartment door. The minute the key entered the lock, though, it swung open forcefully.

"Sorry, this door is so wonky," I said, trying to brush it off. "But, ta da, here it is, my humble abode." We hung our coats and took our boots off before I gave him the grand tour of our tiny bathroom, kitchen, and living room. Jackson wanted to explore every detail, though. He stopped and took in each photograph and painting that was hung on our old cracked walls, and he trailed his fingers along the spines of the books on our shelves.

When he got to all of our crystals in the living room, a bemused smile spread across his face. "Wow, you're really into rocks, huh?" We had quite the collection: amethysts, apophyllite, rose quartz, citrine, kunzite, malachite, any stone a modern witch could want to work with. We used them all for different reasons and rituals and incantations.

I laughed. "I know, so Brooklyn of us. We love them, though." It was easy to pass off our decor as just being trendy and woo-woo. New age spirituality and wellness had become so popular, we didn't have to hide all of our witchy paraphernalia from non-magical suitors and friends.

"They're cool. Especially this guy." He pointed to the large crystal phallus in the corner of the room. Reina had given it to us as a joke at our house-warming party a few years ago. We both laughed as we looked at the oversized, glinting quartz penis.

I poured us each a glass of Montepulciano and we sat on the couch, purposefully angling our bodies toward each other. We clinked glasses before taking a long sip, never breaking eye contact. The rich jammy fruit flavors of the wine danced on my tongue as I searched his beautiful grey eyes. All I wanted to do was kiss him and feel his body next to mine. He was magnetic, pulling me to him, and I was utterly powerless. I set my glass down on the coffee table and leaned into him. I ran my fingers through his light brown hair as I kissed him. His hair was thick and felt like soft straw in my hands. I used my nails to trace along his scalp and he moaned softly as he opened his lips and slipped his tongue inside my mouth.

Jackson wrapped his arms around me, pulling me in closer. His body was warm and sturdy. His hands traveled up and down my back and through my own mane of raven hair. We began to kiss faster and harder, our tongues dancing together, sending a thrill down my spine and between my legs. He guided me onto his lap, and I straddled him as my breasts pushed into his firm chest. I could feel the thunder of his heartbeat. It reverberated from his chest into mine.

We were hungry for each other. He slid his hands underneath my shirt and found my breasts. I moaned as he cupped them gently. I rocked my hips back and forth against his groin and could feel him harden. He used his thumbs to graze my nipples lightly before rubbing them with more deliberateness. I gasped in pleasure, urging him to keep going. Our kissing grew sloppier as desire took over our bodies. He grunted as I grinded my hips against him as he massaged my breasts.

I couldn't take it anymore. I tugged at his shirt, begging for him to take it off so I could feel his skin. Jackson let out a soft chuckle at my efforts before pulling his flannel off over his head to reveal his broad chest. It was taut and defined without being intimidating. He had a swathe of soft curly brown chest hair across his pecks. I ran my hands across his chest, letting the hair fall through my fingers. I played with the tight curls as I admired his figure. He smiled at me bemused. "You have a thing for chest hair?" he asked.

"It's so sexy," I said before returning to kiss him. He gave me one soft kiss before steadying me with his hands.

"I want to see you now," he said. I nodded. He lifted my shirt up over my head, revealing my black lace bra. His eyes glazed over in longing as he retraced his thumbs against each stiff pink nipple peeking through the lace of my bra. I let out a small sigh. Every inch of my body was humming, and with every touch, I felt more charged. Jackson reached behind me and unclasped my bra, exposing my pale breasts. He gasped as he admired them, first with his eyes and then with his hands. He massaged and squeezed them hungrily as he kissed me feverishly before popping one rosy nipple into his mouth. He sucked lightly then harder, swirling his tongue around. A surge of pleasure undulated through my body, and I threw my head back as I let out a breathy moan.

I looked down to meet Jackson's gaze, which was affixed to me. He moved to my other nipple, squeezing it between his forefinger and thumb before taking it into his mouth. I ran my fingers through his hair as he nibbled on my hard nipple, never breaking eye contact with me. I had never been so turned on in my life. I knew I must be soaking wet underneath my jeans. And I could feel him stiff and bulging underneath me as I pulled his face up to kiss me. His mouth was so warm and sweet; his kisses were addicting. I needed more. We continued to kiss passionately as our hips rocked back and forth at a steady pace. I wanted him inside me, though. I *needed* him inside me. I'd never wanted a man more. My hands traveled down to the button of his jeans, but as I began to unbutton them, he grabbed my hands in his.

"Wait," he whispered. I pulled back, thrown off.

"Wait?" I asked in confusion.

"I don't want to rush this," he said.

What? Was I being turned down? Did he not want me the way I wanted him? My mind began to rush, trying to make sense of the situation. Every sign had pointed to him wanting to sleep with me. I thought he was feeling what I was feeling.

"Violet," he said softly. "Please don't be upset. Trust me, I want you. I want you so badly, but I like you."

"Okay…"

"I don't want this to be just sex. I really do like you," he said. Was he bullshitting me? Was this a line?

"Well if you like me, then why don't you want to sleep with me?" I asked. I tried to tone down the frustration in my voice. I didn't want him to think I just wanted to get laid, because I really did like him and feel a connection. But I also really wanted to have sex with him. I climbed off his lap and grabbed my shirt, pulling it back on over my head.

"Because sex means something to me, and I want to make sure we don't rush into anything. I want you to know I want more than just a one night stand."

"Really?" I asked, narrowing my eyes at him. "Is that a line?"

"God, no! Violet, please, believe me. And if you don't believe me, let me prove it to you." His silver eyes widened pleadingly. He reached out and grabbed my hand. It felt so small in his hand. I immediately felt safe when he held it though. I took a deep inhale and closed my eyes, centering myself.

"Okay, I believe you." I looked at him and he smiled sweetly.

"Good, because I really feel something special between us, and I don't think it's just me."

I sighed. "It's not just you. I feel it too."

He wrapped me in his arms, his chest still bare and radiating heat. He embraced me tightly, and my mind began to quiet.

CHAPTER FIVE

When I was 14, my parents got divorced. Their last fight left a scar so deep in me, I hadn't been sure I would ever be able to heal.

It was the last night the three of us were all together in my childhood home. I sat at the top of the stairs, out of sight and crouched into a ball, my arms wrapped around myself in comfort as I listened to them verbally spar.

"Enough! Enough with the coven and the rituals and the moon and your crystals and elixirs and whatever other fucking crazy shit you get into with your friends. I needed you tonight at that dinner. Do you know how many excuses I have to make? The partners' wives think you hate them and that affects their husbands' relationships with me, which affects my job, Maeve. My job! Which you'd know nothing about, because when was the last time you even held a job?"

"Fuck you, John! I am so sick of your condescending patriarchal bullshit. I don't care what those wives think about me. Sorry I don't worship at the altar of capitalism like a limp dick lemming."

"I'm sorry I can't just leave my job and live off of magic like you, which by the way brings in zero money. My job is what pays for this house, your life, Violet's life. I work my ass off so you can live comfortably. And what do I get for it? You're ungrateful and lazy and you put zero effort into this marriage."

"No effort?! You're kidding right? John, I have spent my whole adult life serving you. I gave you a child. I cook for you, I clean for you, I suck your goddamn dick!"

"Oh yeah, Maeve? When was the last time you even did that? We haven't had sex in five months. And you barely cook dinner anymore. You're always ordering takeout, which guess what, costs money! Money that I make so that you can do that!"

Our cat Linus nudged me with his head as I absentmindedly pet him. My jaw began to ache, and I realized I was clenching down hard, as if bracing myself to go into battle. I picked up Linus and curled myself around him, burying my face in his orange fur as I held back tears.

Their yelling downstairs got louder, and I heard my dad go into the fridge and pop open a bottle of beer.

"Yeah, keep drinking, John, that'll help," my mom sneered.

"Maybe I wouldn't need to drink if you weren't my wife, Maeve."

"You'd love that, wouldn't you? If I just walked out and you never had to see me again, huh?"

"Yes, actually, I would."

Outside, the wind howled and thrashed against the windows. The glass began to rattle as I buried my face further into Linus, letting my tears soak his fur. He purred softly as my heartbeat grew faster and louder inside my chest. I tried to calm it down by taking deep breaths but panic was already swelling inside me. My parent's fight became muffled as my head began to spin. Suddenly, a jarring crash consumed the house as the windows shattered. Glass shards flew through the air, settling across the carpet. My parents screamed downstairs in shock and confusion as gusts of wind began to tear through the house.

"Now, look what you've done!" my dad shouted.

"It wasn't me! Violet?!" my mom called out.

"Sweetie, are you okay?" My dad's voice then dropped lower as I heard him sneer in a whisper, "You made her this way. She's going to have to deal with this the rest of her life."

"She's probably upset because you're always yelling and never around, John. . . Violet, are you hurt?" My mom appeared at the bottom of the stairs. A small cut was bleeding on her cheek. I erupted into a sob as my parents rushed up to comfort me. They each wrapped their arms around me as I cried, thankful they had finally stopped yelling.

BIANCA and I got off the subway at the Graham L stop and made our way to The Tilted Hollow. It was nestled between warehouses a few blocks away from the hustle and bustle of Graham Avenue, with all of its restaurants, bars, and bodegas. The door to the bar swung open and unveiled a jubilant scene. It was only 8pm, but already underground people of all kinds were laughing and drinking and flirting.

It was just like a normal Brooklyn bar, except that you could bet the majority of its patrons were of the magical persuasion. You wouldn't know by just glancing around, but the Tilted Hollow was a popular underground haunt. Witches, warlocks, demonologists, mediums, psychics, energy casters, exorcists, and lycanthropes mingled freely over overflowing pints of beer and shots of whiskey.

The bar was narrow but deep, with a fireplace at the front and cozy tables with mismatched velvet armchairs in the back. Bianca and I had to weave our way through the crowd waiting to order at the bar and into the back to find the girls. Hattie, Reina, and Sage sat at a corner table chatting animatedly over half-empty wine glasses.

Hattie caught sight of us before the others. "You're here!" she squealed, throwing up her arms in excitement.

We took off our coats and draped them over the empty chairs they'd saved for us. Reina leaned into the group and whispered, "Bianca, your man is here tonight."

"Oh my god, really? Finally," Bianca said.

"He's sitting at the bar, seat closest to us," said Reina, tilting her head in his direction.

"You better make your move, girl!" Hattie said.

I glanced around the table and caught Sage's eye. She smiled and mouthed a *hey*. I smiled and reciprocated with a mouthed *hi*. Her round mossy eyes were lined in bright turquoise liner to match her hair. It was the first time I'd seen her in makeup I realized. She wore a black tank top that exposed her sculpted freckled shoulders.

"Vi, what do you want?" Bianca asked. "I'll grab our drinks so I can chat up hot demonologist."

"Whiskey sour, please."

"You got it." Bianca took a breath, collecting herself, before heading to the bar. Her posture had completely straightened, and she swished her hips back and forth confidently. I'd seen her do this move before, it was her 'I'm on the prowl' walk. She'd taken extra care getting ready tonight, making sure every tendril of platinum hair was perfectly tousled to mimic the effortless sex appeal of beach waves.

I sat down next to Hattie, and she immediately asked about my date with Jackson. It had made it through the grapevine. Bianca must have told them I had a good date with the new barista at Three of Cups.

"I didn't know you were going out with that guy from the coffee shop," said Sage.

I looked at the table and smiled slyly, "Yeah…"

"That guy is hot," piped in Reina. "How did it go?"

Sage's eyes were fixed on me, and my face began to feel hot. I could feel the blood running to my cheeks. I focused my gaze on Reina and Hattie instead. "It was really fun," I said.

"Did you guys hook up?" asked Hattie.

"We made out, but that's it."

"How was it?" asked Reina. They were rapid firing questions at me now. I started to laugh.

"It was really good! He's a good kisser." I couldn't help but smile. I tried to fight it, but I knew I was grinning. Reina and Hattie started squealing in delight.

"You liiiiiike him," teased Reina. I groaned and nodded, burying my face in my hands.

"I do!" I cried out. "And I hate it!" The girls all laughed.

BIANCA HAD MADE her move and was talking to the hot demonologist. His eyes lit up as she spoke and she kept throwing her head back in laughter. She squeezed his bicep flirtily as they talked. I admired how quickly she could accomplish her goals. When Bianca sets out to do something, she does it. I knew she'd be there for the majority of the night.

One drink turned to two which turned to three. By 10pm, a small dance party had begun at the front of the bar by the fireplace. Fire hazard be damned. One of the bartenders had begun to DJ over the soundsystem. Hattie grabbed Reina by the hand and led her onto the dance floor. They begin to twirl and shimmy in time to the music, their faces rosy from the alcohol. Sage looked at me. "So shall we?" she asked, gesturing towards the amoeba of dancing people. I nodded, and she took my hand. It was warm and reassuring. She gave it a little squeeze, and my stomach did a flip.

We joined Hattie and Reina and began to sway to the music. I arched my back and waved my arms in the air to the rhythm. My whole body began to awaken as the music coursed through my veins, into each limb and each finger, each toe. It flowed behind my eyes and pulsed in my chest. It felt like liquid sunshine moving through my body. I moved with unbridled joy, shaking my hips to the beat and tossing my hair around wildly.

Time was stretchy and springy, oozing slowly only to condense in a state of whiplash as songs morphed into each other, their rhythms ebbing and flowing like the phases of the moon. My long hair had become a tangled and matted thicket clinging onto the sweat on the back of my neck. I had to cool down, so I went to the bar to get some water. I chugged two tall glasses of ice water as I sat atop a barstool, catching my breath while watching the dancefloor.

Hattie and Reina were laughing and dancing with

a trio of floppy-haired, hipster-looking guys in skinny pants and vintage t-shirts. Sage was a few paces away from them, dancing with a petite blonde woman in a tight black dress, tights, and combat boots. They were both moving seductively, swaying their hips in time to the beat as they exchanged sly smiles. The blonde woman stepped closer to Sage and whispered something in her ear.

Sage grinned as she listened intently. The woman then gave a quick bite to Sage's earlobe before leaving the dancefloor. I wondered what Sage's earlobe tasted like as she spun around, still smiling and made her way back to our table in the corner. I got up from the barstool, leaving my empty glass on the counter, and followed Sage's turquoise head as it bobbed and weaved through the swirl of happy, tipsy patrons.

"Hey," I said when I got to the table. Sage was putting on her thick army green puffer coat.

"Hey, I'm gonna head out," she said, zipping up her jacket and smiling.

"Do you want company?" I asked hopefully. She smiled but shook her head no.

"I'm actually going back to Mariah's place. Did you see that girl I was dancing with?" I nodded. "She invited me over for a drink, the little minx." She raised her eyebrow for effect. I fought the urge to roll my eyes. Of course she did. My chest felt tight, and I wanted to scream, but swallowed hard instead.

"Have fun, then. Be safe," I said.

"Thanks, Vi." Sage kissed me on the cheek before walking past me and out the bar door with Mariah. I inhaled sharply as the familiar scent of vetiver and lavender filled my nostrils. My cheek still felt warm from her lips.

CHAPTER SIX

Imbolc had arrived, and the coven had planned to do our yearly celebration at Hattie and Reina's apartment. Imbolc marked the halfway point between the winter solstice and the spring equinox. It was a celebration of the coming spring and a time to honor the Celtic goddess Brigid.

Reina and Hattie lived in a beautiful garden apartment in the historic district of Greenpoint. An elderly witch had rented out the ground floor of her towering brownstone to them for a steal. Best of all, they had free range of the backyard, which was a luxury in the city. Their landlord wasn't even around most of the winter, as she left town after Yule and headed to sunny Florida. It didn't matter if you were magical or not, at a certain age, one became inexplicably drawn to Florida.

Bianca and I kicked off our boots and hung our coats in the tiny entrance way that doubled as a mudroom. The woody sweet smell of palo santo mixed with freshly baked bread filled the air, beckoning us to the kitchen. "Hello, hello!" called out Hattie cheerfully as she was opening the oven. She pulled out two steaming loaves of Irish soda bread. Hattie was the most domestically gifted of us. Her culinary skills, magical and otherwise, were unparalleled in the coven.

"That smells delicious," remarked Bianca, as she leaned in to kiss Hattie's flushed cheek. I reached out my hand to covertly break off a piece to nibble, but Hattie quickly swiped it away.

"Let it cool a bit, Vi. You're so impatient," she said teasingly. Sage, who I just caught sight of curled up in the corner of a room with a book, let out a giggle. She flashed me a smile as I gave her a small wave.

"Happy Imbolc, sisters," Reina's voice filled the room as she strode in from her bedroom wearing a long dusky blue velvet gown. "I figured I'd dress up for the occasion," she said with a spin.

"Hot damn," said Sage, setting aside her book and eyeing Reina up and down dramatically. Reina grinned and rocked her hips flirtatiously. She did look fantastic, the velvet draping beautifully from her curves.

"Well, I'm severely underdressed," I said.

"Not at all, you're perfect," said Hattie. She had somehow managed to get flour on her brow. Bianca licked her thumb and erased it. "Thanks, B," said Hattie.

"So shall we?" asked Bianca. We all smiled and nodded eagerly.

Hattie called out, "Brigid, won't you join us for dinner?" Three deliberate knocks rang out. The sound was directionless and seemed to envelop the room.

Reina arched her raven brow and smiled. "She's here," she said in a hushed voice.

"Welcome, Brigid," I said excitedly. "Let's feast!" The girls cheered, and we began our celebration. We each grabbed a candle in sight and held it ceremoniously till it caught flame, working our way around the room until every pillar and taper was lit.

We sat around the old wooden table in Hattie and Reina's tiny dining room, laughing and eating colcannon and a roast chicken Hattie had somehow cooked so perfectly that the skin was crispy and the insides, juicy and tender. Sage continued to fill our glasses with deep red wine, tending to us like a sommelier.

After dinner, Reina handed each of us a small terracotta pot and sachet of wildflower seeds. We sang an old druid hymn to Brigid as we gingerly placed the seeds in the inky potting soil. The faster we sang, the seeds began to sprout and grow, their stems inching upwards until leaves began to unfurl, followed by delicate buds, and finally a rainbow of blooms. We stood in contented silence, admiring our work, until Sage said in a quiet voice, "I love magic." We all began to giggle, drunk on wine and magic and Hattie's cooking.

"Let's go outside," prompted Hattie, laughter still in her voice. We rushed to throw on our boots and coats, bundling up for the cold like excited little kids on a snow day.

As we headed out into the yard, I quickly checked my phone. It lit up with a text notification from Jackson. *Dinner tomorrow night? I'd love to see you again.* A tingle went from the base of my skull all the way into the pit of my stomach. I quickly flashed back to kissing him on the couch and could almost feel his hands on my breasts again. I wanted more. I texted him back, *Absolutely, let's do it,* and put my phone away for the rest of the evening. I couldn't let my excitement for Jackson get in the way of tonight's celebration with the coven.

In the backyard, we gathered around the firepit. We clasped hands and looked to the nightsky as we whispered the incantation in unison. The fire burst to life, the heat from the flames warming my cheeks. We said a prayer to Brigid before letting go to enjoy the bonfire we'd created together. The flames licked the cold winter air, furling and unfurling at a frenetic pace, as it cast an amber glow upon our faces.

A supreme contentment swelled in my chest as I warmed my hands by the fire and admired each of my chosen sisters' beautiful faces. Hattie's large pale blue eyes lit up as she listened to Reina tell a story about a date she went on, her rosy mouth full of laughter and the tip of her nose pink from the frigid air. Reina's thick curly black hair looked like a heavenly crown in the firelight, her almond shaped brown eyes shining as she entertained the girls. Bianca and her enviable pout smirking as she followed along, interjecting here and there with a gasp or giggle, all the while idly twirling a lock of bleached hair. And then there was Sage, her round mossy eyes glinting as she listened to Reina, her heart-shaped mouth curling in bemusement.

Our wine glasses were nearly empty, so I got up from my seat to pour us all some more. I'd lost count of how many glasses we'd drunk, but we were giddy and the wine helped keep us warm. I sat back down and wrapped myself in the thick woolen blanket I'd brought from inside. With my beanie snug on my head and the blanket enveloping me in its shield, only my nose was cold. My insides were warm and happy.

"So, have you all ever played around with sex magic?" Sage asked with that familiar arch of her brow. I hadn't. I had heard of sex magic, of course, and knew that it harvested the energy of pleasure and climax for you to channel into your incantation, charm, or spell. It was a ritual that could be done alone, with a partner, or even a group, but it required true vulnerability and the ability to completely surrender to the moment. You had to completely leave your head and only be in the body for sex magic.

Bianca piped up. "I've experimented, you could say," she said with a devilish grin. News to me. I shared a bedroom wall with her and had no idea.

"Really? How come you never told me?" I asked. She laughed.

"Vi, I wasn't going to knock on your door and

wake you up to say, 'hey girl, I just masturbated furiously in the name of Diana, thought you'd want to know." We all burst out laughing.

"Okay, fair," I said.

"And did it work?" asked Reina.

"No," said Bianca, shaking her head. "I couldn't empty my mind and kept getting distracted. I did cum though. Hard." We continued giggling as Sage raised her glass in honor of the achievement.

"It's hard to do. I've only succeeded a handful of times, no pun intended," Sage said. Her cheeks were bright coral from the freezing nightair and red wine. She looked like a pre-Raphaelite painting, minus the long cascading hair. But her short crop of turquoise fuzz suited her better. "Honestly, though, it's a game changer. I achieved a level of clarity and insight I'd never been able to unlock."

"Huh…" Hattie mused, which only made us snort with laughter at her innocent expression. Hattie was our same age, but often felt like a little sister. She had an air of childlike wonder about her, and her wide eyed gaze often betrayed her desire to seem cool, collected, and unsurprised by things.

"Hattie, don't come near my room tonight. You've been warned," joked Reina.

"Yeah, Vi, if you hear any strange moans coming through the wall tonight, do not be alarmed," Bianca added. I rolled my eyes, but I was intrigued.

"Okay, okay, okay…" I said. "I'd actually like to know more about sex magic." The girls quieted down. I knew they were just as interested and as curious as I was.

Sage took a long sip of her wine. "I have plenty of books on it in the shop, but essentially, you do a ritual however you normally like to do it. I know we all probably have our own style when we practice magic alone, but I like to use my amethyst, labradorite, and kyanite. Oh, and lapis lazuli— that obelisk I gave you all when I first joined the coven is great for this. Because it takes so much power to open my third eye, I need all the support I can get." We were all nodding, laser focused on what she was telling us.

No more joking around, we all wanted to learn from Sage. As a hedge witch practicing on her own, she'd discovered magic that the academy didn't teach us. If there had been a Sex Magic 101, believe me, I would have signed up.

"Do you drink any tinctures or teas?" asked Hattie.

"Mugwort tea helps, but I've been successful without it, too." Sage smiled reassuringly. "I really do think you all should try it. It's really powerful." We all nodded and sipped our wine as we looked into the flames of the dwindling fire. I knew I'd be making sure we weren't out of mugwort when I returned home later.

CHAPTER SEVEN

That night, after Bianca had gone to bed, I rooted around in our cabinet, combing through our collection of teas, herbs, and roots until I found the mugwort. When the kettle began to sing, I threw some into my blue and white china teapot and poured the scalding water over it, letting the steam kiss my face. I inhaled deeply and its earthy aroma filled my nostrils. I patiently let it steep for ten minutes as I gathered my crystals. Amethyst for protection and spiritual connection, labradorite for connection to the spirit realm, kyanite for psychic support, and the lapis lazuli obelisk Sage had gifted me— I needed them all. For extra measure, I added a few rose quartz pyramids and my favorite peachy-hued lemurian seed crystal to help open my heart and connection to higher knowledge.

I strained the mugwort tea, pouring it into my favorite handmade ceramic mug, the one my mother gifted me for Yule a few years ago. Once my bedroom door was closed, I began to take deep and steady breaths as I let my mind quiet. I lit a small bundle of sage and lavender. Its sweet smoke filled the room, and I cracked my two narrow bedroom windows open so that the stagnant and negative energies could escape.

I set the burning bundle on my iridescent abalone shell and began to hold each crystal above it, letting the smoke envelope each stone, cleansing it so that I could imbue each one with a new intention and power— to gain clarity on Jackson and if I was meant to pursue this relationship. Was it just a powerful sexual attraction or more? I didn't want to let my walls down— the walls I'd worked so hard to build since adolescence— if it wasn't right for me.

My makeshift altar sat next to my bed. It was an old wooden table I'd found in my mother's basement. Apparently, my great grandmother had used it for tarot readings. Atop it sat a number of candles— colorful ritual candles I'd accrued from trips to various metaphysical shops and beeswax pillars I burned with my own magic. For this ritual, I wanted to use my beeswax. I held each pillar in my hands and whispered an incantation as the flame burst to life. Soon, the flickering candles bathed the room in a dim amber light.

I slowly undressed, leaving my clothes in a pile on the floor, before sipping the mugwort tea. It was sweet and heady. I emptied the mug and set it aside, then began to arrange my crystals around the bed in an oval. I said a prayer to the goddesses that looked down upon me as I positioned myself in the center of the oval. I laid down and focused on my breath as I ran my hands up and down my naked body.

Each movement tingled my skin. I swirled my fingers around my nipples as they stiffened, then trailed them down my stomach to my groin. I twirled the short tuft of coiled raven hair as blood began to rush downward. My pulse started to throb between my legs. I ran my fingers down to my opening. It was slick and warm. I used my wetness to glide my fingers over my clit, and behind my eyelids, colors whirled and transformed like a kaleidoscope—indigo turned into a fiery orange which then morphed into an electric lavender. My breathing quickened and became more shallow as I pressed harder against myself with every stroke of my fingers.

I slid a finger inside me, and began to gingerly explore. It was snug and velvety. With every touch, my back began to arch more, beckoning me deeper. I kept my eyes closed as I rocked my hips back and forth, digging into my comforter with my free hand, clutching at it as if to steady me. My body was writhing like a serpent as the feeling began to swell inside of me. I rubbed my thumb in small circular motions atop my clit, softly at first and then with more pressure. I felt like a fire was crackling inside of me, the flames licking at my insides ready to burst. As I rode the precipice of my orgasm, towing the line between the realm of the unseen and the material world, my third eye opened. Visions began to appear beneath my eyelids as if I was watching a film.

Jackson's grey eyes appeared in sharp focus before a montage of all the men I'd put up with because I wouldn't get attached began to blur into one another at a rapid pace. I saw every time I'd left a one night stand, satisfied but bored, each nice boy that had asked me out at the academy sincerely but I'd turned down in an effort to remain distant, detached, and safe from hurt.

Then Jackson reappeared, he was holding me and I was flooded with a sense of ease and safety. He was kissing me and running his hands along my pale naked back. He began to blur out of focus as a full milky moon rose above my naked body. A wolf sat beside me with the same silvery eyes Jackson had. I petted the wolf affectionately and it suddenly turned into Jackson.

We both began to walk down a moonlit garden path and the fragrant scent of jasmine and neroli filled my nostrils. We held hands and walked steadily forward, as my belly began to swell. I wrapped my arms around my stomach protectively until a tiny baby appeared in my arms. Jackson and I looked down onto it lovingly. Another baby appeared in Jackson's arms. We continued to walk, as our bodies morphed and aged, with each baby aging alongside us.

I kept a steady rhythm with my hands, and as an orgasm undulated through my body, the figures disappeared into the night. I was panting and sweaty when I opened my eyes to see the perfect stillness of the dimly lit room. I slowly sat up, trying to avoid a head rush, as my breathing returned to normal. I picked up the lapis lazuli obelisk and cupped my hands around it tightly. Jackson was a lycanthrope. And we could have a future together. If that was the path I wanted to take, it was mine to live.

I'd never even met a werewolf before though, at least not to my knowledge. I'd only learned about them at the academy from professors and books. I knew there was something special about Jackson from the moment I first saw him that morning at Three of Cups, but I never imagined it was that he became a wolf every full moon.

CHAPTER EIGHT

Now that I knew Jackson's secret, I didn't feel so confused by his sexual rejection. Well, I guess it wasn't an outright rejection, but it wasn't something I'd experienced before. Not that I had men fawning over me, begging me to sleep with them, but when I wanted sex, I could get it.

Jackson had chosen a rustic pizza place in East Williamsburg for dinner. Jackson was already standing outside the restaurant as I approached. He waved and began walking towards me, his sinewy silhouette framed in the backlight of the bustling street. My heart began to quicken as I imagined running my hands across his shoulders and down his taut arms.

He greeted me with a kiss, his soft lips surprisingly warm. I pressed my entire body into his, luxuriating in his body heat as the air around us began to swirl and tangle my hair. "You look gorgeous," he said as we pulled apart reluctantly and headed inside the restaurant. The alluring aroma of woodfired pizza welcomed us as the hostess sat us at an unfinished wooden table.

WE WERE ENJOYING OUR PIZZAS, a ricotta and sopressata pie drizzled with spicy honey and another one with gorgonzola, arugula, and fig, when Jackson set down his slice with purpose. "So I do have something I want to tell you," Jackson began. "I know you were really thrown off by the other night, but I want you to understand why." I nodded. "I'm not sure if I'm reading into it and it could just be a coincidence, but we did meet at Three of Cups..." I nodded again, but this time gave him a reassuring smile. His expression softened and his sweet lips began to curl upwards. "Okay, so you can see where I'm going with this then, good. . . I'm actually a lycanthrope," he said. Jackson's silvery eyes searched my face for a reaction. I didn't want him to know I already knew, but I also didn't want him to think I was shocked or upset by this confession.

"Oh," I began, with a small pause for effect as if I was processing this information for the first time. "Well, that's fine. I mean I guess I shouldn't be surprised that there's something special about you since you work at Three of Cups."

"You aren't turned off?" he asked.

"No, not at all," I reassured him. "I'm really glad you told me." I took a sharp inhale. "Since we're being open and honest here, then I guess I should tell you that I'm a witch." There. I said it. Something I had never once said to a man on a date. Other than the guys I had slept with at the academy, no man I've dated or been intimate with has ever known that about me.

He smiled and chuckled a little. "I know," he said.

"You know?"

"Yeah, I could smell it on you," he said matter-of-factly.

"Oh, duh," I said. Lycanthropes had a keen sense of smell. I should have known. Suddenly, I was self conscious, though. "What does it smell like?"

Jackson laughed a deep laugh from his belly. "You're so cute when you worry, but really, you don't need to worry. Witches always have a base note of oak moss and lavender." Lavender, something I could always smell on Sage, as if it was emanating from the flesh behind her small pointed ears.

"You speak like it's perfume. A base note of oak moss and lavender," I said.

"Well, scent is complex. And we can smell every nuance, like how you don't just smell of oak moss and lavender. You smell intoxicating, like fresh rose petals and salt air, with a hint of amber and pencil shavings." Jackson's eyes closed in bliss as he inhaled deeply. "And the slightest bit of warm frothed milk."

I didn't know if I should be turned on or taken aback. It felt vulnerable to be read, or smelled, like that. I couldn't smell amber or rose petals on my skin. "Pencil shavings and hot milk? That doesn't sound very sexy," I mused.

"It really is, though. I promise you smell incredibly good," he said, his eyes wide with sincerity.

"Have you ever been with a witch before?" I asked before taking a bite of char-speckled pizza crust.

"Yes, but it wasn't serious," he said.

I finished chewing and took a sip of wine. "So did you not want to have sex because I'm a witch or is there something I'm missing? I have to be honest, I've never been turned down like that before," I said.

"I'm sure you haven't," Jackson said. "But your being a witch has nothing to do with not having sex with you the other night. Believe me, I wanted to, but it isn't that easy."

"And what's not easy exactly?"

"Well, if we had sex, you'd be my mate. We'd be bonded."

"Are you a virgin?" I asked in shock.

Jackson started to laugh and shook his head. "No, I'm not a virgin."

"So then what happened to those mates, if that's what you call them?" I asked.

"They weren't my mates because I didn't have any feelings for them. There's a difference for us lycanthropes when we have sex without any emotional connection or deeper feelings for someone. Culturally, you're only mated if it's someone you love or have the capacity to love. And physiologically, if I mate with someone like that, I'm emotionally bonded to them for life," he explained.

"So you have feelings for me then." I fought the urge to smile but couldn't resist.

Jackson sighed and nodded. "I do indeed."

"Well, that's rather quick," I laughed.

"I know, we wolves are simple creatures. We like what we like and we don't question it. I felt drawn to you the moment I saw and smelled you."

"That's the most romantic thing anyone's ever said to me," I said. We both started laughing, but couldn't contain our moony grins. Is this what falling in love was like? My cheeks began to hurt because I couldn't stop smiling and my heart beat like the bass in a club, reverberating throughout my whole body.

Our laughter quieted down as our empty plates were cleared. Jackson paid the bill and led me by hand out into the night. The air was frigid and I'd forgotten my gloves, but Jackson's hands were warm and protective. I shoved my free hand deep into my coat pocket but it didn't get as toasty as the hand being held by Jackson. He insisted on walking me home even though it would have been quicker for me to take the subway. Neither of us minded the extra time together, and I wasn't sure what would happen when we got to my front door. Of course, I wanted to invite him up to my apartment and rip his clothes off, but it seemed like that would not be in the cards for us tonight.

We talked the whole way home, and when we got to my building, I didn't want to say goodbye. "Do you want to come up?" I asked hopefully.

"I wish I could, but I don't think it's a good idea,"

he said. My face fell. "I really want to, but I need to make sure you fully understand the implications. You would be my mate. It's not like it could be a fling or a one night or even one month or one year thing. If I have sex with you, I will forever be bonded to you." It was a lot, and I could tell Jackson knew it was a lot to put on someone. And it was noble of him to respect those boundaries, but I wanted him. Sure, I wasn't sure if I could fathom a forever with someone, but the idea of being bonded to him forever didn't sound terrible. I'd never been so vulnerable with a man before, and Jackson made it easy. I wasn't afraid or insecure. He felt safe and warm,

"What if I want that though?" I asked, wrapping my arms around his waist. He took my face in his hands, cupping it gingerly with his long slender fingers.

"I don't want you to make that decision lightly," he said. I nodded. "Why don't you come meet my pack this week?"

"Really?" I asked.

"Yeah, you'd need to meet them eventually. And you'd need to be accepted into the family if we were to mate," he said. "And don't worry, I'm not talking about having babies yet," he laughed. I grinned. The thought of having Jackson's grey-eyed babies didn't scare me. Of course, I wasn't ready for that right now, but thinking about a future with him sent a thrill through me that was utterly foreign.

"Okay, I'd love to," I said. He leaned in and kissed me deeply, slowly at first. He parted his soft lips and slipped his warm tongue into my mouth. I met it with mine and pressed my body firmly into his as I reached up and ran my fingers through his thick hair. His hands traveled down my back hungrily as we kissed passionately. He grabbed my ass and squeezed it as he pulled me into him harder.

I could feel him stiffening even between the layers of clothing we had on. My pulse had traveled into the apex of my thighs. I wanted him so badly. I kissed him thirstily, as if he was water and I'd been living in a drought-ridden land. My whole body was on fire with his touch. We began to slow down before we could get carried away. The city street came back into focus, and I remembered I was standing outside my building. I hoped none of my neighbors had watched us making out wildly like horny teenagers.

I unlocked the door to my building, and Jackson gave me a sweet kiss goodbye before disappearing into the night. My head was swirling, and I felt slightly high. I couldn't believe I was falling so fast.

CHAPTER NINE

It was my first time visiting Sage's metaphysical store, Light and Shadow. She'd opened it three years ago with a loan from her father, and business had been steadily increasing ever since. Soothing classical music filled the cozy shop. A few people were milling about, perusing the bookshelves and tarot decks and assortment of crystals, but Sage was entirely focused on me.

She handed me a small stack of books on sex magic. "These are great introductions to it," she said, patting them like a proud parent.

"Perfect," I said. "Thanks so much for helping me."

"Of course! I'm excited for you to explore. I've found sex magic to be really transformative."

"Yeah, I actually tried it out on Imbolc after our party," I confessed sheepishly.

"Oh my god, how did it go?" Sage asked excitedly.

"Really well, actually. I felt like my third eye completely opened and I was hovering above my body."

"That's amazing. I'm so happy it worked out for you," she said smiling. "Do you still want the books?"

"Definitely. I want to keep learning," I said. "And I was actually going to see if you had any books on lycanthropy."

Sage arched her eyebrow, cocking her head to the side. She looked at me quizzically. "Well I wasn't expecting that, but yes, we have a small lycanthropy section." She motioned for me to follow her as she led me deeper into the store. "Right here," she said, pointing to a shelf marked *Shape Shifting*.

"Thanks, this is great." I traced my finger along the books' spines as I studied their titles. *An Ancient History of Lycanthropy, Werewolves: Friends or Foes, Wolves Among Us: The Everyday Guide to Living Amongst Lycanthropes, A Brief Introduction to Lycanthropy, My Year With The Lycanthropes* . . .

Sage watched me carefully. "I have to ask, Vi, what's got you curious about werewolves?"

I looked into her striking green eyes, which were narrowed in concern. I didn't want her judging Jackson before she even met him— *if* she ever met him. Her heart-shaped mouth was pursed.

"Just wanted a refresher. I took a class at the academy on it and had found it really interesting," I said.

She nodded, but didn't look convinced. "Oh, well any of these would probably be a good choice."

"Thanks," I said as I began to pull each title out to flip through their pages.

"Well, take your time. I'm going to go see if any of those customers need help," she said dismissing herself.

I DECIDED ON TWO BOOKS— *Wolves Among Us* and *A Brief Introduction*— and set them aside by the till before perusing the vast selection of crystals. There were long wooden tables lining the shop covered in stones of all colors, shapes, and sizes. Dazzling silvers and milky pinks and emerald greens and enchanting indigos… it was a rainbow smorgasbord of gems. "Here," Sage's voice came from over my shoulder. I turned around to face her. She was holding a long, delicate silver chain with a deep black stone dangling from it.

She carefully slipped it on over my head, letting it hang from my neck. The stone fell between my breasts and immediately made me feel centered. "Obsidian," she stated. "It will keep you safe and grounded, protected from any unwanted energies."

"Thank you," I said. "How much?"

"No, this is a gift," Sage said smiling.

"That's so kind, thank you," I said.

She gingerly reached for the stone. "Mind if I?" she asked. I shook my head no. Then she closed her eyes in concentration, and I knew she was silently saying an incantation, programming the obsidian with her protective powers. I felt a steely coolness come over my body, followed immediately by a reassuring warmth. She opened her eyes to meet my gaze. Her moss-colored eyes smiled back at me. I reached for her nimble hands and clasped my own around hers, giving them two quick squeezes in thanks.

"Did you find the books you were looking for?" she asked.

"Yes, I decided on those two up there," I said, motioning towards the counter where the register sat.

"Great, I can ring you up for those and the sex magic books then if you're ready."

"Okay," I said.

"You're welcome to hang out as long as you want, though. Don't feel like you're being rushed out."

"I don't, but I do need to get going." My shift at the bakery started in an hour and if I didn't leave soon, I'd be late.

I gave her a kiss on the cheek and made my way to the bakery, eager to flip through the pages of my new books behind the counter. Hopefully, it would be a slow shift. I was meeting Jackson's pack that night and wanted to feel somewhat prepared. It was too bad Sage didn't have a book called *So You're Dating A Werewolf*, that would have been really helpful.

CHAPTER TEN

The heavy metal door to the loft swung open and I was greeted by a face remarkably similar to Jackson's. "Welcome, Violet! It's so nice to meet you, I'm Fiona," she said, leaning in to hug me warmly. "I'm Jack's sister." That was obvious. They had the same bright grey eyes that looked like shining pools of liquid silver and the same thick light brown hair. Fiona's was messily tousled, curling at her shoulders. She led me into the airy living space. It was a wide open loft with high ceilings and concrete floors they'd covered in an assortment of shag rugs.

A man with broad, muscular shoulders and short blonde hair was sitting on a worn leather couch. His arms were wrapped around a tanned and toned man with swooping black hair. "This is Gabriel and Desi," introduced Fiona. They both smiled and said hello.

"It's so lovely to meet you," said Desi as he unwrapped himself from Gabriel's arms. He got up and kissed me on each cheek. "You're a little hottie," he said, flirtatiously eyeing me up and down.

"Don't mind him," said Gabriel as he rose from the couch. "We're so excited to meet you." Gabriel gave me a hug. His arms were thick and bulging like tree trunks.

"Well, thank you for the warm welcome," I said as I handed over the bottle of pinot noir I'd picked up on my way over.

"And she brought wine! I love her already," said Desi, grabbing the bottle and carrying it over to the kitchen in the corner of the room. There was so much counter space and even a kitchen island, a true NYC luxury. The loft was huge, and I couldn't help but wonder how much the rent was. Desi uncorked the wine bottle and began pouring it liberally into some stemless wine glasses.

Jackson suddenly appeared in the doorframe of what I presumed was his bedroom. "Hey, Violet," he said, smiling as he crossed the room. He wrapped his arms around me and the butterflies thundered in my stomach. Then he leaned down and gave me a soft kiss on the lips. He tasted like spearmint and smelled like cedar. A forest green sweater clung to his taut chest and torso. I couldn't wait to run my hands along his body later.

"So this is my home sweet home," he said, looking around the cavernous room. The sky was darkening outside the tall windows adorning the brick wall as dusk turned into night. Fiona was making her way methodically around the room, lighting ivory pillar candles along the way.

"I figured we could use some mood lighting," she announced. Desi went over to the front door and switched off the overhead light. Now the loft was awash in golden candlelight. Gabriel turned on a few small vintage-looking lamps that were scattered around the room to brighten it up a little. The room looked as if it were coated in honey. It was so cozy and inviting, I wondered if this was a normal routine for them. I imagined the pack doing this every night before settling in to watch a movie together or make dinner. It reminded me of our coven get-togethers.

Suddenly the front door swung open, almost crashing into the wall. Athena stomped in, her combat boots landing with a thud every step she took. "Oh, we have company," she commented, her eyes narrowing as she surveyed me.

"Yes, and you knew that," Jackson said, rolling his eyes. "Athena, you remember Violet."

"Of course," she said, her burgundy lips curling into a fake saccharine smile. "How could I forget?"

"Be nice," Gabriel warned.

"Don't let her bother you," chimed in Fiona. "She can be so cranky after bartending."

Athena scoffed as she unlaced her boots and kicked them off before disappearing into her bedroom. She reappeared moments later in sweatpants and a cropped sweatshirt that showed off her six pack. She was lean but strong, and she wanted me to know that.

I wasn't going to let her intimidate me, so I just smiled at her as sincerely as I could. "It's so great to see you, Athena," I said. She nodded dismissively.

"Seriously, ignore her," Jackson whispered into my ear. "She likes to think she's the alpha." Her amber eyes flashed towards him. Even though Jackson was whispering, Athena could hear him. Lycanthropes had a keen sense of hearing. The rest of the pack began to laugh uproariously as Athena scowled from the kitchen. She grabbed a bottle of bourbon from their brass bar cart and poured herself a generous amount before taking a swig.

"What's everyone laughing about?" said a soft voice. The most striking woman I'd ever seen came padding out of a bedroom in thick woolen socks and an oversized heather grey sweater that came to her midthigh. She brushed her ice blonde bob out of her face and rubbed her eyes sleepily.

"Malin, meet Violet," said Jackson.

"I'm so sorry, I just woke up from a nap," she said in a slight accent. Malin was so tall, taller than the boys even, she had to bend down to kiss me on each cheek. "Nice to meet you, Violet."

"Nice to meet you, too. You're gorgeous," I said, not being able to help myself. She gave a small laugh, brushing it off. I'm sure she heard it a thousand times a day.

"Malin is a model, a very up-and-coming model from Sweden," explained Desi. "She's going to get us into all the hottest parties one day." Gabriel rolled his eyes next to Desi.

"What do you do, Violet?" asked Malin as she nestled into a crimson armchair.

"That's a good question… right now, I work at a bakery. I'm still trying to figure out what I want to do," I said, a little sheepishly.

Jackson put his arm around me as we sat on the large leather sectional. "Violet's really clever, I have a feeling she'll do great things." He was smiling sincerely. I peered around the room, looking for a change of subject. A number of ceramic sculptures punctuated the loft. Some were tall and squiggly, others squat and bulbous resting on wooden side tables.

"I love the sculptures. They're so cool," I said.

Desi beamed and looked at Gabriel. "They're Gabe's. He's a very talented sculptor," he boasted proudly. Gabriel smiled self-consciously.

"Wow, I've never met a sculptor before. That's so cool," I said. It sounded dumb coming out of my mouth, but I meant it. I really hadn't ever met a sculptor, and I did in fact find it to be very cool. Gabriel was talented, and I was beginning to feel acutely aware of my lack of accomplishments.

"Don't worry, I haven't sold anything yet. I'm still figuring out how to be a working artist," he said, as if reading my mind. I smiled at him. His cobalt blue eyes were kind and reassuring. "Desi is an actor though," Gabriel said, squeezing Desi's knee.

"I just got my SAG card," Desi said as he tilted his pointed chin upwards before taking a dramatic sip of his wine.

"Congrats," I said, not knowing what a SAG card was.

"Honey, it's the Screen Actors Guild," he clarified.

"Oh, wow, that's great." He nodded. "Have you been in anything I would have seen?"

Desi pouted and sighed. "Noooo, sadly. I mean, yes maybe, but right now, I'm just a glorified extra. I've had a couple lines on some sitcoms here and there."

"But he'll nab an Emmy one day," said Fiona. "As you can see, Desi oozes charisma. How can he not?" They all giggled affectionately, even Desi chuckled.

"Yeah, yeah, yeah, Desi will be a movie star, and Jack and I will win a Grammy, and Fiona will be a revered graphic designer, and Malin will score a Lancome deal, and Gabe will sell a sculpture for $400,000 dollars. We're quite the talented pack," growled Athena from the kitchen. She swallowed the last of her bourbon and stalked over to join us in the center of the room. She plopped herself down on the other side of Jackson, letting her hand rest on his thigh. He looked down uncomfortably and removed it. She glared at him annoyed before rolling her eyes.

WE SPENT the next couple hours eating take-out tacos, drinking wine, and talking. They all bounced off of each other so fluidly. I could tell they were like family and so unwaveringly close. Athena still spent a good portion of the evening scowling and sneering at me, but began to ease up the more the pack ragged on her. Jackson was always touching me, whether it was with an arm snuggly wrapped around my shoulders or pulling me in to sit on his lap. He was so affectionate, and I was a little surprised how open he was in front of everyone— not a bad kind of surprised, a good surprised. He wasn't over-the-top with the PDA, but he was confident. I felt like he was proud to have me there, and he wanted everyone to like me.

As we all got looser from the wine, they began to ask me questions about being a witch. "Can you read minds?" asked Desi.

"No," I laughed. "I'm not a psychic."

"Can you turn someone into a toad?" asked Fiona giddily. I laughed harder.

"Absolutely not." Suddenly it became a game.

"Do you fly on broomsticks?" Gabriel asked.

"Nope," I said. "Sadly, we can't fly."

"Do you have a cauldron?" asked Malin with a sly smile.

"Okay, that I do have." Their eyes all widened like little children. "It's not like a big black cauldron I stir over a fire. It's basically a glorified dutch oven for teas and tinctures and brews." I began to giggle at their rapt faces. "It's not a big deal!"

"Violet was a top student at the academy," chimed in Jackson.

"There's an academy?" asked Malin.

"Oh, I've heard of that place! It's not far from where Jack and I grew up, I think. Somewhere in rural Pennsylvania, right?"

"Yes, but there is one in the city, actually. That one is bigger," I explained.

"Oh yeah, I took an acting class with a witch that studied in the city. She was … eccentric," said Desi, as if he were divulging a big secret.

"Yeah, that's not uncommon for us," I said. "But, honestly, I'm really curious about your pack. How did you all find each other?"

They all exchanged smiles before Gabriel piped up. "I'll take this one," he began. "I moved here eight years ago and met Desi at a gay club— literally sniffed him out— and we were mated maybe— what, babe? A month later?" he asked, looking down at Desi, who nodded back. "Yeah so we've been mated for a long time. Then we met Athena at a small underground concert, and not long after that, we ran into Jackson on a full moon in Prospect Park in wolf form. We all became pretty inseparable and moved into this loft. Then when Fiona graduated college, Jackson invited her to move in and join the pack. And Malin smelled it on Fiona at a vintage store in the East Village. She moved in that night and that's how the pack got to where it is now." Gabriel inhaled deeply and smiled absentmindedly, as if getting lost in the nostalgia.

"You left out the part where Jackson and I almost mated," said Athena sourly. She was sitting on a floor cushion, her hands curled around a glass of bourbon.

"Athena, we were never going to mate," Jackson said firmly. "And you know that."

Fiona shifted uncomfortably on the other side of

the leather sectional as Malin awkwardly looked at the floor. Desi took a long sip of wine, his eyes bulging at the drama. I sat there quietly as my face began to grow hot.

"You all are just good friends. And we're all family, and nothing will change that," said Gabriel in an effort to iron out the tension.

"Exactly," agreed Jackson, his warm hand gave my thigh two reassuring squeezes. I pulled my necklace out of the collar of my sweater and began to finger the obsidian talisman, invoking its protection and letting its power flood my being. I closed my eyes briefly, grounding myself, and said a silent 'thank you' to Sage.

LATER THAT NIGHT, we retired to Jackson's bedroom. It had high ceilings and an exposed brick wall with a window looking out onto the street. He had three guitars hung on his wall— one very old and used looking acoustic, a more polished, newer acoustic, and a black and white electric guitar. Underneath them sat a turntable and speakers atop a wooden side table. A slew of milk crates laden with records lined the wall. His bed sat in the middle of the room, its navy blue linen comforter welcoming us. I hadn't checked the time and didn't see a clock anywhere in his room, but it had to be past two am. Next to his bed was a simple white nightstand with a framed family portrait sitting atop it. I walked over and bent down to admire it. It was old; Jackson looked about twelve or thirteen. He had floppy hair with sun bleached streaks and tan, knobby knees. His family stood in front of the ocean in swimsuits, with wide smiling faces and windswept hair, arms all slung around each other.

"You were such a cute kid," I mused.

Jackson came up behind me and wrapped his arms around my shoulders. "We went to Myrtle Beach every summer growing up. We'd wake up at the crack of dawn to drive down to South Carolina and spend a week playing in the sand and waves. It was my favorite part of the year," he said wistfully.

"It sounds so nice. And you all look so happy."

He spun me around and cupped my face in his hands sweetly. "I'm happy now, too," he said as he leaned in and kissed me gently with his soft lips.

Jackson pulled me onto his bed and began to kiss me more deeply. Our mouths parted, and our tongues met gently as he ran his hands up and down my body. I pressed my body into his as he held me tighter. I felt desperate for him, and slipped my hand underneath his sweater, pulling it up over his head. His lips moved to my neck and he began kissing it, desperately licking, sucking, and nibbling as electricity undulated through my body. Jackson trailed his fingers down my torso and underneath my sweater, searching for my nipples. He began to tease them as I moaned and writhed on his bed. He looked up at me with eyes glazed over in desire.

I fumbled for the hem of my sweater, silently begging for him to take it off. He reached for my hands and moved them away so he could peel my sweater off me slowly. I hadn't worn a bra and Jackson's silver eyes danced as he marveled at them before leaning in to kiss me while gently pinching each pale pink nipple. I craved more and began to whimper when he started caressing each bare breast with his lips. He nibbled and sucked each nipple and hiked my skirt up around my waist as if desperate for me. He pulled down my tights, not even bothering to take them off. They clung to my ankles as he slid his hand underneath my lace thong.

He began tracing my tuft of soft curly hair slowly until he reached my clit. He stroked it sweetly, right in that perfect spot. I didn't have to guide him to it; he found me effortlessly. I moaned as he increased the pressure. Ripples of joy ran through my body. Jackson's eyes were fixed on me as his hungry mouth continued to play with my now stiff nipples. He slid a finger into my wetness, then two, and I gasped at the feeling of his hand inside me, those long slender fingers I'd admired. He began to gingerly move his fingers, beckoning me to come for him.

My hips rocked back and forth uncontrollably, their rhythm becoming frantic as he touched me. He gripped my right knee, steadying me as he continued to stroke me, his eyes full of lust as he softly grunted. I reached for him, desperate to make him feel how I was feeling. I wanted to feel his hard cock, to stroke it and kiss it and show him how much I desired him.

As my fingers brushed the front of his jeans, I could feel his erection begging for me. He shook his head no. "This is about you, my sylph," as he thrust inside me faster and harder.

I cried out as an orgasm seized my body, "Jack... I..." I was panting and sweat had begun to cling to my hairline. He grinned triumphantly and kissed me sweetly.

"I love those sounds you make," he said.

"Oh god, I hope I wasn't too loud." I nuzzled my face into his chest, letting the soft coils of hair tickle me.

"These walls are fairly thick, but wolves' hearing is pretty sharp," he teased. I groaned. "They won't care, Violet. I've heard them all have sex plenty of times." He wrapped his arm around me and began to brush his fingers through my hair, lulling me to sleep.

CHAPTER ELEVEN

"Are you really out of the banana cream pies?" whined a woman with stick straight ash blonde hair. She pouted her fuschia over-lined lips performatively, as if that would help. No, I cannot magic a pie for you, no matter how much you beg.

"I'm sorry, ma'am, but we sold the last one about an hour ago," I said.

"Ma'am," she scoffed. I smiled; I knew throwing that out would irk her.

"Can I get you anything else though? We have one blueberry crumble left that's really good."

"Fine," she sighed. "I guess that will have to do." I boxed the crumble up for her and as I was ringing her up, Athena appeared in the doorway. What was she doing here? How did she know where I worked? The last thing I wanted was to be cornered at my job by Athena. The rest of the pack may have liked me, but I had a feeling Athena wasn't overjoyed.

She sashayed inside the bakery, her auburn tresses swaying with every thud of her combat boots. Leather pants clung to her long, shapely legs. "Hey," she said.

"Hello. I'll be with you in just a moment," I said, smiling saccharinely. She glanced at the ash blonde woman and rolled her eyes as I handed back her credit card. The lady took the crumble in hand and strode out of the bakery without a word.

Athena scoped the shop out, eyeing the baked goods in the display case and then perusing the framed articles on the wall. There were write-ups and reviews regaling the bakery and its owner, Ellie Niehaus, self-taught baker extraordinaire. She'd been featured in everything from *The New York Times* to *Vogue*. I admired her, not just for the accolades but for her determination and pure talent. She honed her skill and with laser focus, built a name for herself, and found community in the New York City foodie circle.

"So this is where you work?" Athena finally asked.

"Yep," I said.

"Food looks good," Athena commented.

"It is... can I get you anything?" She shook her head and then exhaled loudly.

"I wanted to come in and apologize for my behavior the other night," she said quickly, as if rushing to get it over with. I looked at her, letting the silence stretch between us. She could sit in that discomfort; there was no world in which Athena would willingly apologize for anything. When she couldn't stand it any longer, she rolled her eyes dramatically. "So like, are we okay?"

I sighed and shrugged. "I guess. I mean I appreciate you apologizing, although I have a hard time believing it's genuine."

Athena's jaw muscle twitched. "Yeah, well it's not exactly my style, but for the good of the pack, I'll do it."

"Ah, so you were put up to this?"

"Maybe… yes. They said I had to play nice from here on out. Everybody really loved you. It's annoying."

I let out a chuckle and nodded. "I'm sure it is."

"But if you hurt Jackson, there will be repercussions," Athena said, her amber eyes laser focused on mine.

"Is that a threat? How cliché," I remarked.

"Of course, it's a threat," she said with another twitch of the jaw. "I live and die for my pack, and Jackson may not have chosen me as a mate, but that doesn't mean I don't care about him."

"I understand," I said.

"Good." We stood facing each other in awkward silence for a moment before she said, "and I'll take a cinnamon roll for the road."

"Great," I said, leaning into the case to grab one. I bagged it and handed it over with a forced smile. "It's on the house."

Athena's eyes narrowed in suspicion. "Thanks… well, bye then." She quickly turned and exited the bakery with a forceful push of the door. I started to laugh at what a strange turn of events. Athena wasn't such an alpha after all.

I WAS CLOSING up the shop as the bars that flanked the bakery began to hum loudly with patrons who were ready to drink after a long day of work. A group of men in button-down shirts and slim cut jeans were huddled together smoking cigarettes. It had been one of those unseasonably warm days in February and all of Brooklyn seemed to be feeling the spring itch.

My phone buzzed with a text. I grabbed it and saw Jackson's name and my heart gave a little flutter. *Hey, you should come by Three of Cups when you're off,* it read. Normally, I wouldn't want to appear too eager and would wait to respond, but I think we were past that artifice by now. I responded with a *Be there soon* and a smiley face emoji. He sent a kissy face which made me smile like a goon. If past-Violet could see present-Violet, she'd be shocked into an early grave.

I quickly stored all the leftover baked goods for tomorrow's day-olds half-off special. The bakery had a loyal following that showed up first thing in the mornings to score a deal. I threw on my oversized vintage plaid blazer and locked up before walking the fifteen minutes to Three of Cups.

The snow banks had all melted from today's balmier weather so the pavement was slick. I dodged puddles as I listened to a true crime podcast until I arrived at Three of Cups. The door swung open in a gust of wind just before I could touch the handle. I was greeted with the sounds of happy hour chatter and an undercurrent of electronic bass. Most of the patrons had traded in their coffee cups for pint glasses. The witch behind the bar looked familiar and smiled at me in recognition. "Hey," she said as she pulled a pint of some local IPA.

"Hi," I said, eyeing the taps.

"Aren't you friends with Sage?"

"Yes, I am. . . Have we met? I'm so sorry, I don't remember," I said apologetically.

"Not really, I just recognized you from the Hollow. I'm Mariah."

"Ohhhh, yes, I remember now. I'm Violet," I said.

"What can I get you, Violet?"

"I'll take a pilsner, please." She nodded and began to carefully pull a pint with a small foamy head. I reached into my bag to grab my credit card so I could start a tab, but suddenly felt a warm hand squeeze my waist.

"Put it on my tab, Mariah," Jackson's gooey baritone voice tickled the air. I turned around to face him as he wrapped his arms around me tightly.

"Hey you," I said and lifted my face up to kiss him. He tasted like peppermint lip balm and lager. Jackson smiled and carried my beer over to a small wooden table in the corner. He pulled my chair out for me, and I raised my eyebrows. "What a gentleman," I flashed him my flirtiest smirk.

"I always try to be," he said, his lips curling mischievously.

"Do you now?"

"Mmm, I try, even when you make it *hard*." We both laughed. I took a long sip of my pilsner as I admired his shimmering grey eyes.

"So everybody loved you the other night," Jackson said.

"Everybody except Athena," I corrected.

"Yeah, well we had a talk with her."

"I know, she came by the bakery today," I said. Jackson didn't look surprised. I knew it had to have been planned.

"How was it?" he asked tentatively, as if bracing himself for the worst.

"Surprisingly, not awful. I think she did her best." Jackson let out a little chuckle.

"Athena's a tough one. I'm sorry about that. We all love her though, even when she makes it difficult. She's family, you know." I nodded in understanding. "And she'll get better, I promise. Even if we have to make her," he added.

"You might have your work cut out for you," I said jokingly.

"Yeah, well, you're worth it," he said as he reached across the table and curled his long fingers around my pale hand. It looked so small and delicate in his. I sighed; I didn't have anything to say to that. Was I worth it or was he making a mistake? I didn't want to end up breaking his heart if I ran away like a coward, like I'd done in the past. There was a reason

I had only dated fuckboys. No feelings, no pain, no guilt. But then every time I looked into his bright grey eyes, my limbs turned to jello and my stomach felt like I'd been thrust into zero gravity.

I twisted my palm to clasp his hand and gave it a squeeze before leaning across the table and planting a gentle kiss on his soft lips. He smiled as I pulled away and took a sip of his lager.

"So the pack had a discussion about you, and we want to welcome you into our family, if you'll have us," Jackson said, shifting in his seat. It was the first time I'd ever seen him look awkward or nervous.

"What exactly does that mean?" I asked, unsure of what the parameters of joining a pack meant. Could they even accept someone who wasn't a lycanthrope? "I'm not a wolf…" Jackson smiled.

"You don't have to be. It just means that you'd be a part of the pack. You'd be welcome to the loft at any time and our loyalties would lie with each other." Jackson paused and took a deep inhaling before continuing, "and it means we could mate."

"Oh," I said with a small smile. My mind quickly flashed to the other night and his hands gripping my hips hungrily. "So we could finally *be* together," I said.

"Yes," he said with a solemn nod that erupted into a grin. "Finally."

"So what happens next? Let's go back to my place then," I said with a laugh. Jackson smirked and chuckled a little.

"Well, do you want to be my mate?" he asked, his

grey eyes wide and glued to me. I couldn't help but smile. He looked so hopeful and pure. All I wanted to do was kiss him and say yes, but my mouth felt frozen shut.

Jackson gave my hand a reassuring squeeze and its warmth traveled up my arms and into my chest. The butterflies began to thunder in my stomach, daring me to say yes. I nodded before the words could fall out. He leaned in and kissed me hard, letting his lips linger firmly on mine. I melted into the kiss and let my worry fade as his strong hands held my face so lovingly. When we finally pulled apart, I felt like the room was spinning in a technicolor swirl and the only steady thing I could focus on was Jackson's grinning face.

"So before we can formally accept you into the pack, we need you to witness our transformation on the full moon," Jackson said. "You need to see us as wolves to truly know us, to truly know me."

"Okay," I said, nodding steadily, trying not to betray my excitement. I had only read about the lycanthropic transfiguration that happened under each full moon. To see one unfold before my very eyes would be thrilling, and maybe a little bit terrifying.

"Violet, I'm going to do everything in my power to make you happy. That's all I can really promise. I'm falling in love with you, and I don't take the decision to mate lightly," he said solemnly. If this was anyone other than Jackson saying these things to me, I'd roll my eyes or laugh or make a run for it and leave the bar in a hurry. It scared me a little to be so vulnerable, to admit that I was falling in love with him too. I thought about him every morning when I woke up and imagined his lips on mine every night before I fell asleep. It was all so cliché, but damn, it felt really good. It was intoxicating.

"Jackson, I'm falling in love, too," I said. It was out there in the open now. I couldn't take it back. Jackson smiled and began to laugh.

"Why do you look so upset then?" He asked. I began to laugh with him as I tried to soften my uncomfortable expression.

"Because I've never felt like this, and it's really scary!"

"I know," Jackson began, "and we can move as slowly as we want. We don't have to become mated yet."

"Jackson! I obviously don't want to wait. I can't take the sexual frustration any longer!" He began to roar with laughter.

"Well, you better not be using me for my body. I have a brain and a heart too, you know," he teased.

"Of course, of course," I said sarcastically. "Who'd do such a thing?"

"Only a real monster," he said as he pulled on my arms, guiding me up from the table and onto his warm and sturdy lap. He wrapped his sinewy arms around my waist and kissed me on the tip of my nose. I gazed into his silvery eyes as I ran my index finger along the bridge of his adorably crooked nose. Jackson pulled me in tighter, nuzzling his face into my neck and raven hair that fell around my shoulders. He breathed in deeply and exhaled slowly. "You smell so good," he murmured. I let out a giggle as I ran my fingers through his thick tawny hair and closed my eyes contentedly. If anyone was staring at us, I didn't care.

CHAPTER TWELVE

Jackson was waiting for me in the doorway to the loft. His face spread wide into a smile. God, how was he this cute every time I saw him?

"Hey, handsome," I said. He wrapped his arms around me and gave me a squeeze before planting a quick kiss on my lips.

"Thanks for coming. I hope you're ready for tonight," he said, leading me into the loft. It was the night of the full moon, and I would have front row seats to their transformation.

The rest of the pack was lounging in the center of the room. Desi and Gabriel were draped on the leather sectional, while Athena sat on the floor consumed by her phone. Malin and Fiona were both in the armchairs, sipping cups of tea. Fiona set down her mug on the coffee table and clambered up to hug me.

"Violet! I'm so glad you're here," she said warmly.

The rest of the pack said their hellos, except for Athena, who couldn't be bothered to even lift her gaze.

"Thank you for inviting me. I know tonight is special. And honestly, I'm honored you're comfortable enough to share it with me," I said. I'd only read about lycanthropic transfiguration and was trying to contain my excitement about the chance to witness it firsthand.

"Of course, we're hoping you'll be family very soon," Gabriel said with a smile, his eyes darting suggestively between Jackson and me. Jackson slung his arm around my shoulder and kissed the top of my head.

"Well, let's hope tonight doesn't scare her off," Jackson joked. The rest of the pack laughed while Athena sat stone-faced, determined to stay absorbed in her phone.

"Violet, do you know what to expect?" Desi asked, sitting up straighter on the couch.

"Jackson told me a bit about it, and I've done some reading," I answered.

"Good enough," Desi said. "I can't imagine there's anything to really fully prepare you for what you'll see. We've lived our whole lives like this, so I don't know what I'd think if I were you, girl."

"I think I can handle it," I said.

"And we'll take good care of you," chimed in Jackson, giving my shoulder a squeeze.

"Yeah, you're in good hands, Violet," assured Fiona.

Athena cleared her throat loudly. She was over the niceties. "Should we get going then?" she asked as she stood up from the floor.

"Okay, I'll get the basket," said Malin as she set down her teacup and disappeared into her bedroom.

"The basket?" I whispered up at Jackson.

He let out a chuckle. "Yeah, to keep our things in so we don't destroy them when we change," he explained. "You'll see."

Malin brought out a large woven basket from her room as everyone began to put on their coats and shoes. When the pack was ready, we left the comfort of the loft and piled into Gabriel's old minivan. The sun was lowering in the sky as he drove us to Prospect Park, which was where they always went for sundown on the Full Moon. It was Brooklyn's largest park and boasted grassy fields and wooded enclaves for the wolves to explore. When we arrived, we headed straight to one of the forested areas of the park. Jackson held my hand as I followed the pack weaving in and out of the spindly trees, until we reached the smallest clearing. Malin set down the basket and checked her phone. "Okay, it's almost sundown," she announced.

Jackson turned to me and kissed me sweetly, his soft lips leaving mine warm and wanting more. "I know you have your own ritual tonight, so once we've turned, you don't have to stick around for long," he said. He gave me a quick hug before he began to undress.

The pack were stripping bare— unzipping their

coats, pulling off their boots, tugging on their sweaters— until they were completely naked. They placed all of their belongings in the basket Malin had brought, and looked at each other with mischievous grins. The sky was no longer pink, but had turned a brilliant shade of indigo. The moon hung low and full above the horizon as the pack began to change in a series of contortions.

I kept my focus on Jackson as his naked human body began to warp. It twisted and turned at odd angles as he morphed towards the frost covered ground. Fur the exact color of his thick light brown hair sprouted from every bit of skin as his crooked nose elongated into a snout. The transformation looked painful, but Jackson remained silent as his human form fully transfigured into that of a wolf. No longer six feet, he trotted up to me on four graceful lupine legs, coming up to my hips. He nudged me affectionately with his cold black nose and I scratched behind his ears like I would a dog. His hair no longer felt like soft straw, it was now a coarse, wiry fur.

Jackson and Fiona looked almost identical in wolf form, and I could only tell the difference between them because Fiona was shorter and slightly leaner. Malin was stark white, her coat evocative of the Nordic snow in which she grew up playing. Desi was slightly speckled, mostly black fur but with tufts of grey poking out randomly along his back. Gabriel was the broadest of the wolves, his rugby-player build still obvious. His fur was beige and shaggy, while Athena's fur was reddish and had a slight wave to it.

I was now surrounded by wolves, the lone human standing tall as the pack circled around me protectively. They were beautiful and strong, moving with precision and agility. Desi and Gabriel began to tumble, playing like puppies together. Jackson stood on his hind legs, placing a furry paw on my shoulder as he licked my cheek. I giggled at the absurdity of the situation. My boyfriend was a werewolf... My brain tried to do the mental gymnastics of balancing his extremely sexy human form with this majestic wolf that stood before me. I now felt the kind of overwhelming affection I felt for the tiny, fluffy pups I'd see being walked around the neighborhood.

Jackson licked my ear leaving a trail of drool, before dropping to the ground and rolling over. I leaned down and gave him a belly rub. He wriggled with happiness, his tail wagging contentedly. Fiona trotted over and followed suit, inviting her belly to be rubbed. Suddenly, each wolf was competing for my attention, nudging me and rolling over and wagging their tails. I couldn't stop laughing but tried my best to pet them all equally.

Athena was the only wolf who didn't join in. She watched at attention, her hackles slightly raised. As I continued to pet them, she began to pace impatiently, until she'd had enough and let out a low bark. The wolves all stood up to face her. Athena threw her head to the side, motioning to the expanse of the park just beyond the wood. Jackson turned to me and gave me one last affectionate nudge of the snout, his grey eyes sparkling in the moonlight. I gave him a little pat on the head, and off they went. The pack moved in unison, picking up their pace until they were at a gallop. They loped across the grassy fields as the Full Moon shone her light on them. They became smaller and smaller figures in the distance, until all that remained of their presence was a chorus of far off howls.

I ran my fingers through my thick raven mane and put my hood up as I headed towards the subway. I texted the girls I would be home soon; they would be eagerly waiting for me so that we could begin our own Full Moon ritual.

ONCE I GOT HOME, we immediately climbed the stairs to the roof. It was an old building, and the roof was unfinished. It didn't have wooden deck flooring or lounge chairs like the newer or remodeled residential buildings, but it was a large open-air space with an unobstructed view of the moon. We stood in awe for a minute, admiring her swollen form and basking in her silver light.

Reina cleared her throat, ready to begin the ritual. "Here," she said, placing a finger atop a bundle of white sage. It caught flame and began to smoke, its sweet earthy scent filling the air. She began to wave the bundle around like a wand, smudging everything with the sacred smoke— each crystal and vial of oil, everything we'd lugged to the roof for the evening. Then she passed the burning sage off to Bianca.

Bianca bowed her head and began to wave the wand around the crown of Reina's curly head, letting the smoke cleanse her. She ran the wand up and down, taking care not to miss an inch of her, before repeating the same pattern on me, Hattie, and Sage. Once the four of us had been smudged, Bianca handed me the bundle of smoking herbs.

I kissed her cold cheek, and began to float the wand around her head, her platinum hair gleaming in the moonlight. I waved the smoke up and down, forwards and backwards, making sure she was thoroughly cleansed. We were leaving behind the energy of before, wiping our slates clean for the night's activities.

"To mother moon and to my sisters," Bianca said, as she raised an amber glass vial. She tipped it back into her mouth, sipping the elixir Hattie had made for the evening. We huddled together as the vial passed from witch to witch, each of us toasting to the moon and the coven before taking a sip of the syrupy elixir. It was thick like molasses and tasted like dirt mixed with black licorice and peppermint.

We formed a circle and clasped hands tightly as we fixed a glamour on the rooftop, so that to the non magical eye, the rest of the ritual would be invisible. A glamour like this was powerful magic, one witch couldn't perform it alone. Only a coven perfectly in tune could do such enchantments without depleting themselves of power for the next few days.

Hattie picked up the tall crystalline selenite tower and placed it in the center of the circle to aid us in connection to the divine feminine energy of the moon. Then she reached into her bag and pulled out five palm-sized clusters of sparkling purple stones. "I offer amethyst to my sisters," she began as she carefully placed each stone in five equidistant points around the selenite tower. "For spiritual connection to the higher plane," she finished, returning to her place in the circle.

"I offer fluorite to my sisters," said Sage, "for clarity and focus." She carefully set down five obelisks swirling in light green and dusky purple next to the amethysts.

"I offer carnelian to my sisters for energy and creativity," said Bianca, as she placed a rich orange tumbled stone in line with each amethyst and fluorite. The crystal grid began to look like a five-pointed star, with the selenite tower at its nexus.

"I offer moonstone to my sisters," said Reina, "for psychic fortitude and strength." She gingerly added five opalescent white stones to the formation.

"And I offer kunzite to my sisters to uplift us with healing love," I said with a smile, placing the pale pink pieces of raw crystal at the ends of the grid. The formation was now complete, a perfect five-pointed star shimmering in the moonlight.

"Hadn't seen that coming," joked Reina, unable to help herself.

"And look who's supposed to be the psychic among us," I said.

"Hey, I don't pry into my friend's lives without their permission," she said with a smile. "But I'm glad to see the ice queen begin to melt a little."

I threw her a small playful eye roll. "Yeah, yeah, yeah…" I said. "Let's keep it moving." I went over to the pile of stuff we'd brought up to the roof and grabbed the old enchanted phonograph my grandmother had passed down to me. With a double snap of my fingers, music began to fill our ears. The song was lush with a steady beat and swirling, soaring strings faded in and out. It was purely instrumental; we could write our own lyrics in our heads if needed. We began to sway back and forth, slowly at first, letting the rhythm infect our bodies. As the song wormed its way from our ears into our limbs and chest, we began moving more wildly.

Hattie's eyes closed as she threw her hands above her head, making artful waves. I arched my back and contorted my body into shapes that felt gooey and ripe. Sage began to roll her head languidly in circles, while Bianca writhed like a serpent as she trailed her fingers along her thighs sensuously. Reina undulated like an ocean wave lapping the side of a dock as she began to sing out in a low "ah." Sage joined her and they began to harmonize, while I reached for a small drum and began to pound my palms into it.

I synced to the thrumming beat, letting my long dark hair fall in my face. I lolled my head back and forth with every thump, letting the hair swish against my drumming fingers. The elixir's effects were now in full swing, as the night swirled around us in dazzling lilacs and indigos. It felt as if we were dancing among the stars, holding court for the moon as she looked on in amusement. The pace of the music picked up and we began to dance harder and more feverishly, until we entered a trance.

When our bodies were aching and slick with sweat, the music began to quiet itself. I swayed back and forth like a pendulum until I became perfectly still.

"Should we tap into the other side tonight?" Reina asked hopefully, her face flushed and shining.

"I'm game," said Sage. The rest of the coven nodded in agreement. We returned to our circle and held hands tightly, heads bowed and eyes closed in reverence. We stood in silence for a few minutes as Reina whispered a prayer under her breath. She was our strongest channeler, as she came from a long line of psychics and mediums.

"Spirits, beloved and missed, do you have any messages for us today?" she asked. We waited in hushed anticipation. Only a few moments passed before Reina inhaled sharply. "Violet, dear," she began in a low raspy voice, the sound of the other side, "the wolf and the undine are calling to you. Choose your path wisely." I knew it had to be my grandmother. She spoke up most often on these full moon nights. And she always had a fondness for speaking in metaphors. I knew who the wolf was, but who was the undine?

Reina exhaled slowly, before taking another sharp inhale. "Mia stellina," said the low voice. Now it was Bianca's nonna's turn. We often had a lot of grandmothers popping in. "Don't ink your body. I know you want, but no good. Molto brutto." Bianca stifled a giggle as Reina let out another long exhale.

A few silent minutes passed as we waited to see if any other messages would be channeled. Reina usually broke the connection if it was radio silence for more than five minutes. Before she could close the channel, that low voice suddenly began speaking, "Sagie, you've grown into such an incredible woman, and I'm so sorry we didn't have more time together. I love you so much, and I'm always with you." Reina let out a deep breath and began to recite her prayer under her breath, closing the door to the other side.

I opened my eyes and looked at Sage. Her mossy eyes were wide and glistening. I wanted to wrap my arms around her and pet her pale turquoise head soothingly. Her mother hadn't sent a message before now, and I'd never wanted to pry and ask Sage if she'd ever worked with a medium or had any contact with her mother on the other side. When Reina finished her prayer, we dropped our hands and rushed to Sage. Hattie wiped away her tears with a gentle hand before enveloping her in a hug. I extended my arms, wrapping them around the both of them, and Bianca and Reina followed suit. Sage sniffled a little as we stood embracing her in our group hug.

"We love you, Sage," said Hattie. The rest of us murmured in agreement.

"Thanks, I love you all, too," she said as her ragged breathing returned to normal. "But I think I'm ready for this hug to be over." We burst into laughter and gave Sage some space as she dried her face with the sleeve of her grey sweatshirt.

CHAPTER THIRTEEN

I woke to see Sage's turquoise fuzz dappled in the morning sun. She'd ended up crashing at our place instead of taking the subway home exhausted in the wee hours of the morning.

She was curled up on her side, her back to me. Her hands were clutching the white comforter as if she was protecting herself from the monster under the bed. The steady rise and fall of her breathing filled the quiet room. I didn't want to wake her, so I tried to slip out of bed as carefully as I could, but she began to stir. Shit.

"Hey," Sage said sleepily, turning over to face me. Her eyelids were heavy from dreaming.

"Sorry," I whispered.

"No, you're fine. I slept really well. Thanks for letting me crash." She raised her arms up and began to stretch, waking her body.

"Of course," I said, sitting back down on the bed. "How are you feeling?"

She let out a sigh. "I don't know. Good? I think?" She paused for a moment. "I wasn't expecting my mother to be channelled, so I was a little thrown off, I guess."

"I get that," I said. "You probably felt pretty vulnerable."

Sage nodded. "Oh yeah, but everyone was so nice about it."

"Well, yeah of course. That's what friends do, what *sisters* do," I said.

"Yeah, I guess I'm still adjusting to that, being on my own for so long. You can take the witch out of the hedge… or something like that," she joked lightly.

"Oh, right," I said quietly. It was so easy to forget Sage hadn't always been a part of the coven; she fit in so seamlessly with the rest of us. I'd never had to practice magic alone, had never been a hedge witch. As a young girl, I had my mother, her coven, Bianca, and my grandmother, and after high school, I went to the academy and was surrounded by witches. Magic and community and friendship had always been intertwined in my life. I couldn't think of one without thinking of the other.

"Ah, I don't mean to be a bummer," she said, her voice buoyant. "Don't look so sad, c'mon."

"My stupid face, I can't ever just let my emotions hide in peace!" I laughed.

"Well, it's a pretty cute stupid face at least." Sage flashed a flirtatious smirk. I playfully rolled my eyes.

. . .

THAT AFTERNOON, after Sage had left for work, Bianca threw the kettle on to make us tea. It had been a little while since we'd had some quality time, just the two of us. "Caffeine or herbal?" she asked as she held the cupboard doors open, scanning our abundance of teas.

"Caffeine, definitely," I said.

"Earl Grey?" Her long red-lacquered fingertip coaxed the blue tin of earl grey off the shelf. She didn't wait for me to say yes.

"I'll get the milk," I offered, turning to the fridge.

"Great." Bianca grabbed a porcelain teapot with hand painted lilac blooms and scooped a generous amount of loose tea into it. She always made her tea strong, and I always needed a lot of milk.

When the kettle began to whistle and shake, she turned off the gas and poured the steaming water into the teapot. The smell of bergamot filled the air. I took a deep breath, luxuriating in its scent. Our kitchen had a small wooden table and two mismatched wicker chairs that caught the best light from the room's lone window. Bianca set down the pot, two mugs, and the strainer, and I added the small porcelain creamer that matched the teapot.

We sat across from each other, and Bianca poured each of us our tea over the strainer, letting the stray leaves catch in its mesh. I poured a generous amount of milk and watched as it swirled and bloomed in the dark amber tea. Bianca drank her tea black. "Like my heart," was a favorite joke of hers.

I reached for the tarot deck we kept on the

windowsill next to our little table and removed the hunk of clear quartz atop it. "Should we read some tarot?" I asked. Bianca nodded. I bowed my head and silently said a blessing as I began to shuffle the cards.

"Draw a single card," I prompted Bianca, as I fanned the deck towards her. Her eyes darted from card to card, until settling on one. She waved her hand slowly above it as it began to peel away from the deck. The card fell to the table and Bianca flipped it over. Four of Wands. Two figures adorned in flowers were shown, celebrating with arms raised underneath four wooden pillars— the wands— that were also brimming with flowers. Bianca let a small smile creep across her face as she took a sip of her tea.

"A new relationship is coming, and you can enjoy the fruits of your labors. You've built this community around you— duh— and it's time to celebrate together and bring new love into your life," I said as I studied the card.

"Hot demonologist," she smirked. "I guess I should start calling him Derek."

"That's not the name I was expecting," I joked. "Not very mystical."

"No. But he *is* hot." I let out a little laugh. Bianca pointed to the deck. "Your turn. Draw a card."

I fanned the deck across the table and closed my eyes, letting my hand explore the energy radiating from the cards. My fingertips began to feel hot suddenly, so I quickly pulled the card underneath. I opened my eyes as I turned it over. The Moon. A wolf sat next to a pool of water, beneath the full moon, its head thrown towards the sky as if howling. I looked up at Bianca, she was studying me with a furrowed brow.

"The moon sheds light on what is unseen. I need to let myself follow my instincts because an emotional decision is going to need to be made," I said quietly.

"And there's a wolf," Bianca said. "What's going on with wolves, Vi? Your grandmother said something about a wolf last night, too. What aren't you telling me?" Her chocolate eyes narrowed and held my gaze. She knew I was hiding something from her. I shifted in my seat as I searched for the right words.

"Jackson isn't fully human…" I trailed off, Bianca nodded impatiently. "He's a lycanthrope."

"Guess I should have seen that coming," Bianca joked. "And how are you feeling about that? Are you worried at all?"

"No," I said, shaking my head. "I'm not worried, he's not feral. He's lived his whole life with a pack, first his family and now his friends in Bushwick."

"So those rumors are true, then, there *is* a pack of werewolves in Bushwick." I nodded. "So if you're not conflicted about that, what's going on? Do you like him?"

I grinned uncontrollably, rolling my eyes at myself. "Yes, I really like him. Like more than I've ever liked any man in my life. He's kind and smart and a good kisser and so cute and sexy and he plays guitar and is a good friend and brother." Bianca began to laugh. "What? Why are you laughing??" I asked.

"You're so fucked," she said with a smile. "I've never seen you like this, Vi. You've always been our ice queen and now you've gone and melted. Just like Reina said. . . You're in love with this dude. You're in love with a lycanthrope from Bushwick. I can't." She giggled into her tea, and I groaned.

"Ugh, I know, I know! It's like I don't recognize myself or any of these feelings, and it's really scary. . . but it also feels so freaking good, B." Bianca set down her mug and reached across to my hand. She gave it a reassuring squeeze.

"I know, Vi," she said, her face softening. "But this is a good thing." I nodded. "I want to meet him. I get it if you don't want to get the coven involved yet, but I really want to meet him, Violet. He's gotta be pretty special if he's got you in this state," she smirked affectionately.

"Yeah, I know I've already met his pack and it's time for him to meet ours I guess," I said.

"Mhmm," sighed Bianca with a smile.

She took a sip of her tea and then arched her brow mischievously. "And how's the sex? Is it different banging a werewolf?" She giggled and flashed me a naughty grin.

"So that's the other thing."

"Oh no," Bianca said, her eyes wide.

"No, no, no, everything's been really, *really* good. We just haven't had sex yet. We'll be mated when we do," I said. Bianca looked puzzled.

"Mated? Like you're going to have to have his babies?"

I rolled my eyes and shook my head. "No, god, somehow us witches can be so ignorant of other underground people. Mated is a kind of bonding. It's a commitment, both physical and emotional, that lycanthropes make when they fall in love," I explained.

"Oh, so like he'd be your boyfriend?"

"Yeah, I guess that's a good way to put it. Just a little more intense since I think it has some more physiological consequences for him."

"Are you worried at all?" she asked.

"No, not worried. Jackson is so special, and I want to be with him. . . It's just that this is all so foreign. Like, even if he was a normal guy or a witch, I'd be navigating uncharted waters," I said. I took a sip of my tea and searched Bianca's face for answers. She was always so great at giving me advice, why couldn't she just tell me what to do now?

"So you're just uncomfortable that you're actually developing an emotional attachment to him?" She let out a soft laugh. "Look, I get that it's scary and vulnerable to like someone and fall in love and trust them, but it's one of the most beautiful parts of life."

"I know. . ." I trailed off.

"But?" Bianca arched her brow.

"What if I get hurt? Or worse, I hurt him." I could feel tears forming in my eyes and tried blinking frantically to ward them off. A small smile spread across Bianca's face as she leaned a hand across the table and began to gently wipe away the tears. I let them fall as she continued to erase them. She got up from her seat and came over to hug me.

"It's going to be okay. You might get hurt, and you might hurt him. Even if you end up together for the rest of your lives, there will be pain sometimes. That's just how life goes. You can't hide from it, Vi," she said tenderly. Her arms held me the way my mother's would when I'd get upset as a kid. My muscles relaxed, and I let myself sink into her arms with a heavy sigh.

"You're right, I know. You're always right," I said.

"Yeah. . . I am, aren't I?" she said teasingly.

CHAPTER FOURTEEN

I need to see you. I sent the simple text into the ether as my heart pounded. Outside, the sun was lowering swiftly, turning the sky a burnt orange and then deepening to an inky cobalt.

Bianca had made me feel supported and safe, like I didn't need to be afraid of what I was feeling and what I wanted so badly. Love might be a freefall, but at least Bianca and my coven were sturdy and reliable parachutes. They'd make sure I landed safely.

My phone vibrated. *On my way.* Jackson only lived about twenty to thirty minutes away, depending on the trains.

Bianca stood in her room with the door open. She was in front of her dresser, gazing into the mirror while meticulously painting her lips a ruby red. "He's coming over now," I said from the couch in our tiny living room.

"Okay, so I'll meet him, we can have a drink, and

then I'm going to head out and meet Derek," she said as she carefully checked herself out in the mirror.

I took three deep breaths to calm my jitters before going into my room to make sure everything was clean. I fluffed my pillows on the bed, put away the stray tubes of lip balm and crystals strewn across my dresser and nightstand. My reflection caught my attention, and I leaned in to inspect myself. My hazel eyes looked more golden than usual. I wiped a few stray flakes of mascara from underneath my eyes, but otherwise, I looked fine. My lips were plump and smooth with a creamy sheen of rose-colored lipstick and my brows were perfectly filled in with black powder. I adjusted the delicate gold chains that hung around my neck. I liked the way the lone silver chain from Sage stood out, the black obsidian glinting between my breasts.

Bianca had moved into the living room and begun lighting candles. "I'm setting the mood for you two," she called out. I smiled to myself as the butterflies flitted against the sides of my stomach.

"Thanks," I said. I passed through the living room and into the kitchen to grab a bottle of wine. "Which one should I open?" I asked.

"Maybe the sauvignon blanc. It's light and flirty," Bianca said. She came into the room and pulled three wine glasses out of the cupboard. I poured us each a generous amount.

Bianca raised her glass towards me and cleared her throat dramatically. "To the official melting of my favorite ice queen and to falling in love," she said. I raised my glass to meet hers with a clink before taking a long sip, letting the bright grapefruit and herbaceous notes fill my mouth.

The front door buzzer rang out, startling us. "He's here," I said to Bianca. My eyes felt like they were bulging out of my head. She laughed and pressed the button to let him in the building. We listened in giddy anticipation for his knock. A minute later, it sounded out. Bianca gave me a wink as I went to open the door.

"Hey." Jackson stood in the doorway. His eyebrows were raised as if in concern, but his lips were in a slight smile.

I grabbed him and wrapped my arms around him tightly. He softened as he stretched his strong arms around me, cradling my head with one of his hands. "Hi," I said into his warm chest. All of my nerves melted at his touch.

"Invite the man in," Bianca said from the kitchen. He laughed. I stepped back and looked into his bright grey eyes and led him inside.

"Jackson, this is Bianca. Bianca, Jackson," I said. Bianca smiled as Jackson stepped forward and shook her hand.

"Hi Jackson, it's nice to meet you," Bianca said warmly. Her eyes lingered on his taut chest peeking out from the opening of his coat. I stifled a giggle.

"Pleasure to meet you, Bianca. I've heard a lot about you," Jackson said.

I took his coat and hung it up by the door as Bianca poured him a glass of wine.

"Hope you like sauv blanc," said Bianca, handing him a dangerously full glass.

"I do. That's quite a generous pour," he remarked with a smirk.

"Well, I didn't know how much liquid courage you might be in need of — I know I can be intimidating to some men," joked Bianca. I rolled my eyes.

"Don't worry about her, Jack, she's a softie underneath it all," I said, giving his arm a flirtatious squeeze.

We brought our glasses into the living room and settled in. Jackson and I sat on the couch, his arm confidently draped around my shoulders as he sipped his wine. Bianca fired questions at him from the blue velvet armchair. After the obligatory getting-to-know-you questions, she shifted in her seat and took a long sip of wine.

"Okay, Jackson, I feel like I need to address this, and I hope you don't take any offense, but what's with this whole mating thing?" Her brown eyes were laser focused on Jackson's reaction.

"You don't have to answer that," I cut in. Bianca was fearless, and I didn't know if I admired her in that moment or thought she was incredibly rude.

"No, it's okay, I understand. I don't mind talking about it," said Jackson. He rubbed his thumb against my shoulder reassuringly.

"I'm just looking out for Vi," Bianca said.

"I get it," he said. "I know it sounds intense. But I really care about Violet. Mating would mean we were bonded for life. It doesn't mean we have to stay together forever," he said, glancing down at me, his silver eyes shining. "But we would always have a connection, an emotional and psychological link to one another."

Bianca's eyes narrowed. "And what exactly does that mean?"

"Well, it's not really an exact science, but say if we're apart and Violet has a really bad day or feels a very strong emotion, I would begin to feel that emotion without any context and know something was upsetting her." Jackson took a sip of wine. He was calm, but I was studying Bianca. Her face began to soften.

"Okay," she said with a sigh.

"You good?" I asked her. I tried to put as much levity in my voice as I could.

"I'm good," she said nodding. She drank her wine and watched us in silence for a moment. "I like you, Jackson," she declared. He laughed.

"Great, glad we cleared that up," I smirked.

"I'm gonna head out and meet Derek for dinner." Bianca set down her empty wine glass and grabbed her coat by the door. I got up and followed her into the kitchen. She gave me a firm hug and whispered into my ear, "I really like him for you." I smiled and mouthed *me too* as she zipped up her coat.

"Have a good night, and great meeting you, Jackson!" she called out into the living room before striding out the door.

"She really liked you," I said, as I plopped back down onto the couch next to Jackson.

"I know, I heard," he said with a smirk.

"Right, you sneaky wolf," I said as I trailed a fingertip down his bicep.

"I liked her too," he said.

"She's great, isn't she? I knew you would."

I leaned into him, a whiff of cedar filling my nostrils. He cupped my face in his hands as he pressed his soft lips into mine.

He kissed me with such care, I melted into him like snow on a sunny day. His long fingers held my face tenderly as our lips met and our tongues danced passionately. I ran my hands across his strong shoulders and down his firm arms, the bulge of his bicep sending an extra thrill down my spine. I traced my fingers along the hem of his t-shirt before pulling it up over his head. He peeled my sweater off and tossed it aside as I unhooked my bra. I pressed my breasts into his chest as I kissed him hard and ran my fingers through his thick tawny hair.

Jackson trailed his fingertips down my back and around my waist to the front of my jeans. He unbuttoned them and quickly tugged them to the floor. I giggled and pulled his pants off him. He grunted and kissed me as he ran one hand through my raven hair and grabbed my ass with the other. Our bodies pushed into each other as if in desperation for the other. His cock was protruding stiffly into my abdomen. I could practically feel his heartbeat as we kissed, increasing at a breakneck pace as I steered him towards my bedroom, never parting with his soft lips.

He wrapped his arms around my hips and set me on the bed. I gasped in anticipation as he looked at me with glossy, hungry eyes. "Jackson," I murmured softly as he began to slide my navy lace thong down my thighs. He kissed me and spread my legs open with his strong hands.

"Let me make you feel good," he whispered. He smiled and eagerly dove between my legs, taking me in his mouth. I moaned as he licked and sucked and swirled his tongue around, slowly at first and then faster, softer and then harder.

The window flew open with a gust as the ripples of pleasure traveled up my spine and down my thighs all the way to my toes, which were curling uncontrollably. He forcefully grabbed a hold of the soft flesh on my hips to steady me against his mouth. He pressed his tongue firmly into me as my back arched and undulated frantically with mounting pressure. My moans grew louder and breathier until I burst, my thighs shaking spastically as I came. Jackson kissed the milky white fat of my inner thigh and smiled up at me proudly.

"You taste incredible, like sweet citrus," he said. "I could eat you for dinner every night." He gave a playful soft bite to my thigh, and I giggled as I pulled him up to kiss me. I poured all of my desire into the kiss as I began to stroke him. He was thick and rigid with excitement. I sighed contentedly as I touched him, and he let out a little groan of pleasure.

"Sit on the edge of the bed," I said. He nodded as I kneeled on the carpet before him. He was beautiful.

Every muscle, every curve and angle of his body, every hair, every vein, every scar, every freckle, every blemish, I feasted on him with my eyes as he played with my hardened nipples. I ran my hands along his sinewy body, down his firm torso and onto his taut thighs, which I gripped as I took him in my mouth. He gasped. "Violet . . ." he groaned as his head rolled back in pleasure. I licked and sucked and teased him, as his groans and sighs and grunts delighted me. I began to twirl my finger in the coarse curls between his legs as I explored every inch of him with my mouth.

Jackson began to pant and before I could take him over the edge, he pulled me off of him and up to meet him on the bed where he kissed me passionately. He wrapped me tightly in his arms as our bodies rocked back and forth against each other, in time to a silent beat only we could hear. I moaned and sighed, begging him to enter me.

"I want you inside of me," I said. He kissed me hard as he rolled us around the bed.

"I love you, Violet. I want to be mated with you," he said, his voice low and breathy.

"I love you too, Jackson. I want that too. I've never felt like this before," I said, overcome with emotion, the words waterfalling out of my mouth. I looked into his bright grey eyes before kissing him sweetly on the lips as he pushed into me. We gasped. He filled me and my body began to soar. Air began rushing in from the window, whirling around the bed as if we were sailing on the ocean. We began to frantically make love, desperate to be as close as our physical bodies could get to one another. I'd never had sex like this before. . . affection and desire and love swelled in my chest and stretched through each limb as I wrapped my arms around Jackson's broad back.

Pleasure surged through my body, pulsing in waves with each stroke. Our tongues and bodies intertwined as our breathing became quicker and shallower. I rocked my hips back and forth into Jackson harder and faster until I began to whimper, tears streaming down my face, as I burst at the seams. An orgasm tore through my body as I moaned loudly through our kiss. Jackson began to grunt as his muscles tensed up and seized momentarily before he relaxed and fell into me. He released a groan that met my moaning midair as another orgasm undulated through my body.

Jackson slowly rolled off of me and enveloped me in his arms so that we lay on our sides facing each other. We were both shiny with sweat as the gusty wind slowed to a cooling breeze. We kissed sweetly and gazed into each other's eyes in comfortable silence. Jackson smiled as his breathing returned to normal. "My beautiful sylph," he murmured lovingly as the breeze danced across his flushed face. "I love you so much."

"I love you," I said with a smile. He reached across and tenderly tucked a lock of my hair behind my ear.

"My mate," he mused dreamily.

"So does this make me . . . your girlfriend?" I asked coyly. He laughed.

"Of course, Violet. You silly witch," he said teasingly before kissing me sweetly.

I sighed as exhaustion and happiness flooded me. Our bodies stayed intertwined as the night grew quiet, and we drifted off into a heavy sleep.

CHAPTER FIFTEEN

Bianca had invited the coven over under the guise of a movie night, but really she wanted me to come clean about Jackson to the girls. Now that we were mated, I couldn't play coy anymore. "We don't keep secrets," she had admonished. And as usual, she was right.

The girls entered the apartment like a force of buoyant energy. Sage, Reina, and Hattie were midconversation, laughing and chatting animatedly. They each embraced Bianca and I warmly before unzipping and unbuttoning their jackets and kicking off their boots.

"Vi, your skin looks amazing," Reina commented. Hattie and Sage studied my face and concurred.

"Yeah, you're glowing," added Hattie. Bianca flashed me a knowing smile.

"Gotta love rosehip oil," I said, brushing it off.

Bianca began mixing cocktails in the kitchen as

the rest of the girls settled into the living room. "I'm making palomas with mezcal," she announced.

"Yum, sounds delicious," said Sage as she plopped onto the faded pink couch.

I set out a bowl of chips and salsa on the coffee table and turned on the bluetooth speaker. "What's the vibe?" I surveyed the girls.

"Something a little lush but chill," said Sage.

"No downers," added Hattie. I put Sylvan Esso on shuffle. They all murmured in approval.

"Palomas are ready," announced Bianca from the kitchen. I went to help her carry them in and handed a drink to Sage, who brushed my fingertips as she took the glass. She slyly smirked up at me, and I quickly looked away.

I settled onto the floor cushion, folding my legs in a pretzel shape, and took a sip of the smoky grape-fruit cocktail. It reminded me of summers spent watching the sunset from our roof. I could almost feel the warmth of the humid July air.

"So, I think Violet has something to share," Bianca said, directing everyone's attention towards me. She shot me an encouraging look, but all I could do was respond with a sigh.

"Gee, thanks for putting me on the spot, B." Hattie, Reina, and Sage were nestled into the couch, their limbs affectionately intertwined as they nursed their drinks. They looked at me expectantly. "Okay, so you know how I had been dating that guy Jackson, the barista from Three of Cups?" They all nodded, and Hattie began to grin excitedly. I felt my lips begin curling into a smile as I tried to fight it and remain blasé. "Well he's kind of my boyfriend now." I said quickly, letting the smile spread across my face. Hattie and Reina cheered and squealed, but Sage remained quiet, her face unreadable.

"And...?" prompted Bianca, her dark eyebrows raised high.

"And he's a lycanthrope..." Their mouths dropped open in surprise.

"What?!" cried Hattie, her pale blue eyes shining.

"Hot," mused Reina.

Sage scoffed, but wouldn't meet my gaze. "I knew something was off about that guy."

I chose to ignore her dig, as Reina asked how the sex was, typical Reina.

"So we actually only just had it. . . because we became mated," I said as my cheeks flushed. I couldn't stop smiling, and I felt oddly embarrassed. Not of the fact that I had a boyfriend or that he was a lycanthrope, but that I was fawning over a guy. The old Violet would be in utter shock if she saw me now. Hattie and Reina giggled at my discomfort affectionately.

"Vi, I have never seen you like this. And I kinda like it," teased Reina.

"So. . . how was it??" Hattie asked excitedly, her eyes ever wider than normal.

"Incredible," I sighed. Hattie squealed and Reina whooped. Sage sat on the couch, her lips pursed. She looked like she was suppressing a scowl.

"So when do we get to meet him then? This is a

big deal, girl!" Reina said as she dug a chip into the salsa.

"Let's all go to The Tilted Hollow tomorrow," said Bianca. Reina and Hattie both cried out in agreement as they nodded their heads enthusiastically.

"I cannot believe you are in love! Finally! The first time in your life, Vi!" Hattie looked at me as if she was proud of me. It made me giggle. She was such a hopeless romantic.

"No more ice queen," remarked Reina in amazement.

"I am but a puddle," I joked.

"Are you sure it's safe?" Sage said quietly from the couch. The room suddenly felt as if she had sucked all of the air out of it.

"Huh?" I asked, taken aback.

"I mean, he's a werewolf. A lycanthrope. Are you sure it's safe to date him?" she asked. The question was meant to sound caring, but it was tinged with disdain. What was up her ass? I didn't act this way when she went home with Mariah, who had been a total stranger.

"Yeah, he's not dangerous. He's a good man," I said. I crunched down on a chip and munched my frustration away.

"I really liked him," chimed in Bianca. "He seems good for Violet." Hattie grinned and Reina nodded approvingly. Sage looked unconvinced.

"Well I can't wait to meet him," said Reina.

"Same," added Hattie.

We all tucked into the chips and salsa for a

moment, and I was happy to no longer have all the attention on me. It was the first time I felt awkward around Sage, and I didn't like it. Why did she have to push so hard on the werewolf thing? I hadn't taken her to be such a judgmental person.

"So, should we watch a movie then?" asked Bianca. She turned on the television and began scrolling through Netflix.

"Let's watch something scary," said Reina.

"Oh, yeah, we can turn off the lights and get spooky," giggled Hattie.

"I'll light some candles," I said, grabbing the box of matches on the coffee table.

"Yes! Use that rose one I picked up the other day. It smells divine," said Bianca, gesturing to a pale pink glass candle on the bookshelf.

I opened up the matchbook to see one lone match left inside. "Shit, we're out of matches. I'm gonna run to the bodega and get some more," I said.

"Why don't you just use magic?" asked Reina.

"I'm too tired," I said. The girls all nodded in understanding. Magic was a renewable resource; I couldn't harness it if I was feeling depleted or lackluster.

"I'll come with," offered Sage, getting up to grab her coat.

"You don't have to, it's just on the corner."

"I don't mind," she said as she buttoned up her mustard peacoat. I shrugged as I zipped up my puffy jacket.

"We'll be right back," I said to the girls as we headed out the door.

We walked in silence down the street. Clusters of people passed us as they chattered, probably heading to or from the bar. We passed a tapas restaurant that was full of people smiling and drinking wine in dim light.

The bodega's fluorescent lights illuminated the corner of the sidewalk in front of the storefront. Sage quickly took two paces ahead of me and opened the door for us. "Thanks," I mumbled. I weaved through the narrow aisles until I found a big 100 pack of matches. A couple of guys in baseball hats were ordering sandwiches from the deli counter and began to check us out as we scooted by them. I plopped the matches down on the counter and gave the cashier my card.

"Minimum's $5 for credit cards. This box of matches is $3.50," the cashier said sternly.

Sage quickly grabbed four single dollar bills from her coat pocket before I could dig around my own bag. "Here, keep the change," she said with a smile. He nodded. Why was she suddenly being so nice?

I threw the box into my bag and headed back into the cold night air, Sage at my heels.

"Violet," Sage said. I turned around to face her as we stood on the corner. Her round moss-colored eyes shone like glowing orbs in the dark.

"What?" I said. I could hear the annoyance in my voice, and I tried to swallow it. Sage looked at me silently, her eyes searching my face. "What?" I repeated, this time in a whisper.

She stepped towards me and quickly cupped my face in her cold hands as she pressed her lips against mine. That heart shaped mouth that I'd admired since I'd met her was now kissing me. The world began to spin. The lights from the bodega seemed to strobe as the sights and sounds of the Greenpoint night swirled around us.

At first I was stunned, but I began to melt into her and kiss her back. I wrapped my arms around her as she pulled me closer to her. Her lips were soft and luscious, and I could taste the smoky mezcal on her from earlier.

A siren wailed as an ambulance approached, washing us in its blue and red lights. I stepped away from her as the street came back into focus. The ambulance sped by as we both stood there, looking at each other quietly.

"I needed to know what it felt like to kiss you before I miss out completely," Sage said. Her face was soft and pleading. I stood there frozen on the sidewalk feeling as if the air had been knocked out of me. "Violet. . ." she trailed off as she looked at me expectantly, willing me to say something.

"I. . . Why did you do this now? Why couldn't you have kissed me before I met Jackson?" My voice trembled, and I couldn't tell if I was angry or wanted to cry. "I'm with Jackson now, Sage. I'm in *love* with him."

"I'm sorry, I just . . . I don't know. I'm sorry. I don't want to stand in the way of your happiness."

"You were being so cold earlier. It didn't seem like you gave a damn about my happiness."

"I was upset and jealous. It wasn't my best moment, I'm sorry." Sage's voice cracked as she looked down at the dirty pavement.

I opened my mouth as if to say something, but no words came out. I didn't know what to say; I was confused and frustrated. Guilt began to sneak up on me as I realized how much this could hurt Jackson if he knew. It was just a kiss, sure, but I was his mate now. And Sage wasn't *just* a friend.

Silently, I turned on my foot and began to walk towards the apartment. Sage followed me the whole way back to the apartment, past the tapas restaurant and up the old cracked marble stairs, without saying a word.

CHAPTER SIXTEEN

That night I couldn't sleep. I'd doze off for an hour or two only to be awoken by my own tossing and turning, the sheets underneath me damp with sweat. The evening's events kept playing in my head on repeat, as if I was stuck in a time loop. I couldn't shake it. I tried drinking more and that only made me queezier. If I thought too much about Jackson, I felt like I was going to throw up. I began imagining him having caught me kissing Sage like that and feeling so betrayed. I had just given him my whole heart, and look at how I was treating his heart. . . and why did I kiss her back? I didn't need to wrap her in my arms and hold our embrace for as long as I did. Her kiss was so warm and soft. It was sweet and pulled me in like an undertow. We didn't speak the rest of the night. I sat on the floor, drinking at a steady pace as we watched some slasher film from the 80s. Sage was curled up on the couch. She didn't make her usual jokes or running commentary. I don't know if the girls had noticed, but thank god, nobody said anything.

Eventually I got up, slick with sweat, and padded across the apartment and into the bathroom. I gripped the sides of the toilet as I dry heaved, willing myself to retch. With the alcohol out of my body, I sipped on some water from the tap as I stood in the silent dark kitchen. I glanced at the clock; it was 3:00AM, the witching hour ironically. Jackson would be meeting the rest of the coven, including Sage, later today. . . would she play nice? I was determined to make sure he felt comfortable and welcomed by my friends, not judged or scrutinized skeptically.

I set down my empty water glass and headed back to bed. I pulled the covers around me like a cocoon and began to take long, deep breaths until I finally faded off to sleep. A strange dream took hold of me. I was in Three of Cups with Sage, on the caramel leather couch. She leaned in and we began to kiss. Then she began to morph into Jackson. I continued to kiss him, letting his strong arms envelope me. Sage suddenly appeared next to us on the couch and whispered something nonsensical in my ear as I kissed Jackson. She grabbed me by the neck, pulling me away from him. Jackson stood up, and they began to fight. They were yelling and snarling and hurling punches maniacally as I screamed at them to stop. They couldn't hear me and my body began fading into invisibility. Nobody could see me.

I woke up confused, the sheets tangled around me like restraints. The sun was streaming in from the window, and I could hear the faint sound of birds chirping from the treetops in the neighbor's yard. It took me a moment to realize I was alone and in my bed. For a second, I thought I was in my childhood bedroom, waking up early on a Saturday morning before my parents. I half expected Linus to jump up and cuddle me.

I could hear Bianca cooking breakfast in the kitchen, so I got up to join her. She looked at me funnily. "Everything okay?" she asked.

"Yeah, just weird dreams. . ." I opened the fridge and grabbed the orange juice. "Want some juice?"

"No thanks, I'm making scrambled eggs, though. Want some?"

"Yeah, that would be great, thanks." I poured myself a tall glass of juice and chugged it as if it was bringing me back to life.

"You excited for tonight?" Bianca asked.

"Um. . . maybe?" Bianca laughed affectionately as she hovered over the stove. "I just hope everyone gets along."

"I'm sure they will. . . I noticed Sage was a little off last night," she remarked.

"You noticed it too, right? It wasn't just me?" I perked up, relieved I hadn't just been extra sensitive.

"Yeah, she didn't seem like her normal, happy self. Do you know what that was about? Is she okay?"

I shrugged. "No idea. . . maybe just an off night." A pang of guilt flickered in my chest as I refrained from telling Bianca about Sage and my kiss. I could hear her in the back of my head saying *'We don't keep secrets.'*

I STOOD outside The Tilted Hollow, waiting for Jackson. He rounded the corner and grinned. I ran up to him excitedly and we kissed. "Hey you," I said. "Ready to meet everyone?"

"Yeah, I'm excited," he said as he nodded and squeezed my hand. I led him inside and we wound our way around clusters of people drinking and talking until we got to the table with the girls. They looked like four queens holding court, ready to welcome their loyal subjects. Their spines were straight, hair brushed, drinks full— ready for action.

"Hey everyone, this is Jackson." They all smiled and began to say hello as I introduced each girl. "And this is Hattie, Reina, Sage, and of course, you already know Bianca." I looked up into his bright grey eyes as he nodded and greeted each of my friends warmly. He was so effortlessly friendly and easygoing. I felt a surge of pride. Yes, this was *my* boyfriend, *my* mate.

Hattie and Reina got up to hug him. Reina let her hand linger a moment too long on the curve of Jackson's bicep as she winked teasingly at me. Hattie began to ask him about his music and his family, as Reina nodded along, interjecting here and there with funny remarks. I admired their natural charm as they talked with ease, entertaining Jackson while still taking the care to actually learn about him. Watching my friends and Jack bond like this filled me with a warm fuzziness, and I hadn't even had a drink yet.

I glanced at Sage, her eyes were trained on me. She quickly looked away, avoiding eye contact with me. Bianca got up to give me a hug, and Sage reluctantly did as well, I'm sure so she wouldn't look unfriendly or strange.

"They already love him," mused Bianca as she hugged me. I nodded with a smile.

"Hey," said Sage as she stepped next to Bianca.

"Hey," I said. Bianca looked at me and made a face as she side eyed Sage.

"I'm gonna run to the bathroom," she announced, dismissing herself from the awkward tension.

"Mariah's coming in a bit," Sage offered.

"Oh. . . okay." Was she trying to upstage me bringing Jackson into the fold or was I reading into this?

"What? That's okay, right?" Her voice was soft. I was bracing for defensiveness, but there was none. Her round green eyes shone in the bar light as she looked at me sincerely. She really wanted to make sure it was okay. I felt my shoulders drop, as if I had been holding them in anticipation for a spat.

"Of course. I just didn't realize it was more than a one-night thing," I said.

"Yeah, it just kind of happened. . ." We stood quietly, both of us nodding awkwardly. I wanted to laugh. Sage and I had never had this dynamic before, it was very weird.

Jackson swiveled and joined our conversation, or

lack thereof. "Hey, Sage, I've seen you around the coffee shop. You have the coolest hair," he said.

"Thanks," she said with a small smile. "It's great to meet you." Well, I guess she was trying to be polite at least.

"Sage actually owns that shop Light and Shadow. It's where I got those books on lycanthropy."

"Ohhh, very cool. Thanks for helping educate my girlfriend," Jackson joked. I smiled at his goofy grin. He was so freaking cute.

"Of course, happy to help." Sage was watching me, as if studying me to see how I looked at Jackson and how I acted around him. I squeezed his shoulder as he looked down at me with his silver eyes.

"Ah, let me get us some drinks. Sage, need anything?" Sage shook her head no. "Vi, do you want wine? Liquor? Beer?"

"I'll just have a beer, whatever you're getting, thanks." He smiled and headed to the counter to order.

"He seems really nice," said Sage. If this was the best she could do, I'll take it for now.

"Yeah, he is." I said with a smile.

JACKSON and I stood huddled by the bar, waiting for our second drinks. He was holding my hand as our heads bopped along to the dance music playing over the speakers. He gave my hand a squeeze and leaned in to me.

"Hey, so I wanted to make sure you were okay

last night?" His eyebrows were arched in concern. Shit. I guess this was part of that mate connection. . .

"Yeah, I just wasn't feeling too hot," I said, brushing it off.

"Are you sure? I could feel something was. . . off. I know this is new but you can talk to me about anything."

"Yeah, I know, I just drank too much, that's all." I flashed him a smile that I hope was reassuring before leaning in to give him a soft kiss on the lips. "See? All good?"

He smiled and nodded. "All good. I really like your friends."

"They're the best, aren't they?"

We stood there holding hands, waiting for our beers and watching the dance floor action.

It was late enough now that the dancing amoeba of people crowded at the front of the bar had begun to grow and mutate. Sweaty people would leave it to grab their next drink or chug ice water while newly liquored up patrons would weave their way onto the dancefloor. Bianca, Hattie, and Reina had just joined the throng of dancing bodies, their faces flushed and smiling. Hattie caught sight of me and waved, motioning for us to join them. I nodded and mouthed *in a minute*. Sage entered the dancefloor not long after, Mariah in tow. They were holding hands and giggling. Sage wrapped her lithe arms around Mariah as they swayed. Mariah swished her hips as she got down to the beat. Sage eyed her lustfully and cheered her on.

"We should join them," Jackson said. He was smiling and laughing as he watched them.

"Definitely," I said. The bartender finally handed us our beers. We cheersed to each other, Jackson's silver eyes gleaming. I leaned in and kissed him. "I love you," I said.

"I love you, my little sylph. Now let's see that ass on the dancefloor," he said with a little playful pat on my rear. I giggled and led him into the crowd where we joined all the girls dancing. Jackson turned on his toes and moved his hips side to side, goofily showing off his dance moves for the girls. They all laughed and egged him on. My cheeks hurt from smiling as I twirled and teased Jackson with my hips, pushing them out rhythmically. He wrapped his arms around me, pulling me into him, and the rest of the dancefloor melted away. It was just Jackson and me, swaying in time to the beat.

ACKNOWLEDGMENTS

A big thank you to Madeline Concannon, my editor and Cancer queen. I am so grateful for your support and sharp eye.

Thank you to Naomi and Paige for reading my unedited raw materials and encouraging me with your honest and funny reactions. I kept chugging along because you two gave me that feedback I so desperately needed (oh, how I wish I could write in an echoless void, but alas).

To all my friends who never stop cheering me on, thank you, thank you, thank you: Joanna, Rebecca, Hayley, Christina, Taylor, Morgan, Chantel, Sydney, Kara, Danielle, Heather, and Jamie.

Thank you to Roman Belopolsky, my chosen brother and favorite critic, for your cover design, dedicated eye, and unabashed opinions and counsel over the years.

And of course, thank you to my parents, Bob and

Cathy, for your love, support, and always letting me talk openly about sex without it being weird. I couldn't have written this book without you two.

I love each and every person mentioned with so much fervor, I feel I could burst.

ABOUT THE AUTHOR

Kit lives in Greenpoint, Brooklyn with her scruffy rescue dog, Cricket. When not writing, she's dancing around her kitchen unironically to Lana Del Rey, pining for Van Leeuwen pistachio ice cream, or soaking in the bathtub until devastatingly shriveled.

Sign up for her mailing list at kitearnshaw.com to stay up to date with new releases.

instagram.com/kit.earnshaw

Made in the USA
Coppell, TX
24 May 2021

56232179R00100